STONE COVE
ISLAND

STONE COVE
ISLAND

SUZANNE MYERS

Published in the United States by Soho Teen
an imprint of
Soho Press, Inc.
853 Broadway
New York, NY 10003

Library of Congress Cataloging-in-Publication Data
Myers, Suzanne
Stone Cove Island / Suzanne Myers.

HC ISBN 978-1-61695-437-6
PB ISBN 978-1-61695-575-5
eISBN 978-1-61695-438-3
1. Mystery and detective stories. 2. Islands—Fiction.
3. New England—Fiction.] I. Title.
PZ7.M9917St 2014
[Fic]—dc23   2014019051

Interior design by Janine Agro, Soho Press, Inc.

Printed in the United States of America

10 9 8 7 6 5 4 3 2 1

For my mother, who always thought I should be a writer

PROLOGUE
WHAT HAPPENED TO BESS

It was my fault that she was murdered. The night Bess died, she left the bar at the marina late. She would have had a couple of drinks, not enough to get drunk. She would have danced, maybe with Jimmy, maybe with Nate, maybe with an older guy we didn't know. She would have walked home alone. Unless I was sleeping over, she always went home alone. She was mad at me that night. I knew that, but I couldn't help it. I couldn't go out.

I got into bed early but couldn't sleep. My skin was itching and my ears were ringing. I was probably still awake while it was happening. Bess always told me to snap out of it, that it was just one of my moods and I needed to get hold of myself. But when I looked in the mirror, I saw black hollows that should have been my eyes. My skin was puffed and pale. I was so ugly. I couldn't stand the idea of people looking at me. I needed to be alone, where no one could see me. So I couldn't go to The Slip with Bess.

The Slip was our diviest bar, and not the atmospheric kind of divey. There were wobbly plastic deck chairs, sticky folding poker tables. The finish on the floor had worn off, replaced with a years-deep varnish of soaked-in beer. Someone had strung some thick, knotted rope around the walls in a lazy nod to the nautical theme. It was gross, but they didn't card there. In town, the bars had to protect themselves. They had the summer tourist business to worry about. It was way too risky getting busted for letting kids in. But tourists would never make it out to The Slip, so no one there ever paid attention.

Sometime after midnight, Bess would have left.

I went over and over it in my head, realizing I'd never know the real story. It wasn't far to the bungalow she shared with her mom, halfway between the marina and East Beach. She might have had that lame Phil Collins song stuck in her head. We hated that song so much. We used to sing it to each other as a joke, howling into hairbrush handles and making gooney faces like we were in some lame romantic comedy, then collapsing in hysterics on Bess's bed.

Or maybe—and I preferred this version—she had been singing that Sinéad O'Connor song she loved. Bess had a nice voice. The song was everywhere that summer, about how all the flowers had died when Mama went away. Bess loved the way that "Mama" was wedged into the line like an upbeat afterthought. She thought it sounded like a bubble popping. She was good like that at describing things. After she pointed that out, I could never hear the song any other way.

Bess had been too good a swimmer to drown. I don't mean too good a swimmer to get caught in a riptide; she was too good a swimmer to go swimming alone on a moonless night in the remorseless Atlantic Ocean. She was smart and she was sensible.

Her clothes were found in the lighthouse, covered in blood. Her killer had cut off all her hair. Some people said a huge anchor had been painted across the front door of her house. Others said that was only a rumor. I wouldn't know; I didn't go to her house again after that night. Her body was never found.

Her mother, Karen, refused to talk about Bess afterward. She got rid of all her stuff. I wanted to keep something to remember her, but Karen said no. Maybe she knew what I knew: Bess had been scared before she died. She had shown me—just me, she swore— the letter.

I only read it once. I didn't copy any of it down. But I can still remember every word. "Uninvited guest," it began and then later, "down came a blackbird and pecked off her nose." The more I tried to push that line from my mind, the more fiercely it returned, and with it her face. I hoped he had not done anything to her face.

I should have gone with Bess to The Slip that night. I should have told someone about the letter. But I never did.

ONE

Of course we knew that Hurricane Victor was going to be a big storm. But there hadn't been a storm like this in anyone's living memory, so we weren't prepared for the damage it would do.

I live on a small island a few miles off Cape Ann, about an hour north of Boston. Our closest mainland towns are Rockport and Gloucester. When you grow up on an unprotected island facing Atlantic storms, you're supposed to know what to do when things get serious. But we'd had so many false alarms, so many calls to evacuate to the mainland, only to return to find no damage or, much worse, that thieves had taken advantage of a day they knew they could work pretty much undisturbed. No one on Stone Cove Island evacuated for a storm warning anymore.

The morning after, I opened the front door to find a fifty-foot oak tree lying across our porch. I squeezed through the narrow gap the tree allowed and stood outside. Its trunk came up to my waist. The island was silent, as though all the sound had been sucked away by the force of the hurricane as it ripped through. There were no birds chirping, no insects. I couldn't even hear the waves, though I could imagine how wild the ocean must be.

I *could* hear my mom, banging pots and dishes inside as she worked herself into a panic, trying to figure out how to make breakfast in a kitchen with no power or water. She was the oatmeal-and-eggs type, not the cold-cereal type, and definitely not the roll-with-the-changes type. Dad was asleep. He'd been up all night, moving furniture up to the second floor as the water rose, trying to make extra sandbags out of freezer bags and flour, taping and re-taping the windows as the wind sucked the glass in and out.

Who knew glass could bend like that? The porch light lit the pea-soup-green night, and the trees screamed as they blew sideways. No wonder the big oak had come down. It was amazing more trees hadn't. I didn't think I'd be able to sleep, but I'd finally nodded off on the floor in my room, well away from any outside wall. My bed and the rug in my room were soaked. The rain had poured under the closed bottom window forming a waterfall, as if someone was holding a hose to the glass. I was scared, but I knew my dad was busy doing all he could to keep the house together, and my mom would make me more freaked out, not less. So I just lay there, waiting for it to be over. I tried pretending it was tomorrow already, and that all this was behind me.

"Eliza?" I could hear my mom calling me from the kitchen.

"I'm out front, Mom. Just checking things out." I didn't mention the oak. My dad's best at handling bad news with her. "I'm going to walk into town and see how everyone is.

Maybe they have power. Do you want me to get coffee or anything if they have it? Or more bottled water?" She was a worrier, so bottled water was one thing I was pretty sure we had plenty of.

"Eliza, no. I don't want you going out there alone," she called back. The clattering in the kitchen was getting more frantic.

"It's fine, Mom. The storm's over."

"What if a branch falls? It's not safe for you to be out there. Nate?"

I heard my father's exhausted voice from the next room. "Let her go. She's fine. Eliza, walk down the middle of the streets, stay out of the park and don't go near the water. Get extra batteries from Harney's if he's not sold out." Then he rolled over and went back to sleep, or so I guessed. It was a familiar pattern: Mom, looking for a reason to panic; Dad, reeling her back in. I hadn't figured out his magic formula. Usually my attempts to calm her down only made things worse.

I turned my attention back to the oak and to how I was going to get off the porch. The trunk was wide and blocked my view of everything beyond it. I was dreading what I would find on the other side, but putting it off would only make my imagination run wild. It was better to face it, however bad things might be, then figure out what to do next.

I threaded my way to the edge of the porch, grabbed a sturdy branch, climbed out and dropped to the ground. It wasn't that difficult, but coming and going this way would not work with groceries. The bay window off the kitchen would have to become our temporary entrance, unless Dad wanted to get into it with the back door. Its seized-up lock hadn't worked since I had been in fourth grade. I looked out at the formerly cozy little street, and felt like Dorothy landing in Oz.

SUMMER IS OUR BIG season. Growing up on the island, you get used to the time before Fourth of July and the time after. It's like living on two different planets. In the off-season, you can ride your bike across the whole island until your fingers are frozen to the handlebars and not see another person. There is only one school with about forty kids in each grade. We all go there, our parents went there, and mostly their parents did too. The ferry runs once a day and when the harbor is iced over, there are lots of weeks it doesn't run at all.

In the summer, crowds stream off the ferries hourly. They juggle beach chairs, umbrellas, Radio Flyer wagons packed with groceries for their summer rentals. The inn is full. People pack Water Street, the main drag that curves along the harbor, wearing bathing suits under their T-shirts and sundresses, licking their dripping ice-cream cones. By the way, don't ever let anyone talk you into working in an ice-cream parlor as a summer job. It sounds fun, but it's actually grueling, charley-horse-inducing work. I always go for day camp counselor: sailing, Capture the Flag, and campfire songs.

You would think summer would be our total focus, that we would be holed up like hibernating bears waiting for beach weather, but it's not like that at all. You get used to the silence and sense of belonging that we few residents have. It's like throwing a party. You're excited before, decorating and getting things ready. It's fun while the party lasts, but eventually you just want the guests to go home so you can put on your pajamas and sit around the kitchen, rehashing the highlights.

That morning, Stone Cove Island didn't look like any version of itself I'd ever seen before, summer or winter. Our street was smothered with downed trees and broken branches. It would be a while before any cars could make it through. My dad had said to stick to the middle of the roads, but I had to zigzag around or climb over whatever blocked my way. I couldn't choose the path. I turned down the hill toward Water Street, my breath catching in my throat. It felt like watching a movie about someone else's ruined life. Houses were missing roofs, walls were caved in. In some cases, only the rubble of the brick foundation was left. Furniture, clothes and belongings were scattered everywhere.

Those personal things tugged at me the most: the stuffed tiger that no doubt some toddler was unable to sleep without; the royal-blue leather family photo album, assembled over decades and destroyed in one night. I pulled my sleeves down over my hands and folded my arms across my stomach. It was cold, and I felt the chill in the small of my back. I wished I had not come down to face this alone.

When I reached the harbor, normally the busiest section of town, I kept my eyes on the water. The beach had ugly, deep gashes in it, like a monster had bitten away hunks of flesh and left bleeding mud behind. I tried to put it back together in my mind to the way it was supposed to look, but I couldn't. Tears began to sting my eyes. I felt the destruction, as though I was the one who had been hurt.

Where the ferry came in—or used to come in—the docks were all but gone. The few weekend people who hadn't made it over in time to prepare for the storm were rewarded by having their sailboats either washed up and overturned on the village green, a hundred yards from the water, or shattered into kindling-sized strips, floating beside the broken pilings they'd once been secured to.

The village green was charred a yellow brown, the grass burned by the salt water that had flooded it. The shops that were on the bay side of Water Street were either gone or ripped open like dollhouses, their sun hats and saltwater taffy boxes floating in murky, possibly electrified standing water. Businesses on the up-island side of the street fared a little better. At least the water had receded.

The whole island seemed to be without power except for the Picnic Basket, the sandwich and coffee shop on Laurel Lane. Nancy and Greg appeared to have rigged a generator. I could smell coffee brewing and theirs were the only lights glowing on the main street. So they'd been lucky too. I felt a quick rush of relief. If the Picnic Basket were dark, I would have panicked. Nancy and Greg were known to be the source of all news, official and unofficial, on the island. They prided themselves on always being first to know. They were also usually first to gossip. The Picnic Basket was probably the nerve center for Hurricane Victor information by now.

I wiped my tears with the sleeve of my sweater just in time to hear my name.

"Eliza? Is that you?"

When I turned, Charlie Pender was standing behind me.

What is he doing here? That was my first thought. Charlie had graduated from Stone Cove High last December, a semester early. I had not seen him since. I remembered that he was taking a year off before college to intern at a newspaper in Boston or Providence and wondered if he might be on some kind of assignment. He seemed taller, or maybe it was just because I felt so beaten down that morning. I saw that same feeling reflected in his eyes; they were faraway, cloudy. In fact, he looked like he was in the same state I was—dazed, distracted, his sandy hair unbrushed, dressed in dark jeans, a sweatshirt, and low-top black Converse. That was funny: we had the same shoes on. But I could feel the space he'd put between himself and the island. It made him seem like a stranger.

Of course, there had always been some distance. While he and I were friendly, our families weren't. That is, my mom and Charlie's mom made clear their lack of interest in being friends. His parents owned the Anchor Inn, one of the oldest and definitely the biggest of the hotels. They lived by the success of the island as a summer destination. My mom thought Cat Pender was manipulative, a "climber," she called her, always sucking up to the richest guests at the inn. I didn't know what Cat thought of Mom, but I could easily project my own complaints: too nervous, too shrinking, too fragile. My dad and Charlie's dad were neutral at best. As one of the few local contractors, my dad often worked on projects at the inn, but I don't think they'd ever so much as shared a beer.

"This is crazy, huh? Everyone okay at your house?" He sounded wired and a little scared, just like how I felt.

We hugged hello. I was glad for the company, even if he had almost caught me crying.

"Yeah. Big tree came down on the porch. But everyone's fine. This is unbelievable," I said. "How's the inn?"

"It has some damage. That's a pretty exposed spot up there on the hill. My parents are trying to make the best of it. They don't want their guests to panic."

The inn sat on the bluff, perched above the harbor. Every spring it was repainted a perfect, gleaming white. Next door was the famous Anchor Club, known for its grass tennis courts and the croquet tournaments, where members dressed in the white, traditional clothes of the 1920s, when the club was founded. I pictured the howling winds I'd heard the night before, raking through the white clapboard walls, rattling the slate rooftops—as if fighting to tear apart the years of island history. I felt a sinking in my belly. Everything about my life on the island had seemed permanent until last night.

"Are you here to do a story? You're working at a newspaper, right?" I asked.

"The *Boston Globe*. I don't get to write much though. A little for the website but it's mostly research and whatever anyone else doesn't want to do. I was coming back this weekend to see my parents anyway, so I thought I'd stay in case it turned out to be big."

We both took in the mangled shore. It was big.

"I feel bad," he said. "I almost feel like I willed it. Looking for a story."

"Weather's not that mystical," I said, mostly to myself. "It's just weather. This just happened. It's not like we asked for it."

"Huh. You haven't changed. That's nice." I felt a weird flutter as he said it. I didn't know he thought of me as being any particular way. It was uncomfortable, the compliment amid the destruction.

"Yeah, well, I'm still here," I said quickly. "Things don't change that much. You're the one who left for the big city, right?"

"True," he said. He looked at me a minute, like he was going to say something else. "Should we go see what's going on? Nancy and Greg have probably set up a war room down there."

"Or at least they'll have some coffee." I'd been drinking coffee, black, since I was twelve and hanging around my dad's construction sites. My mom didn't know about it until much later. Of course she disapproved. My feet were wet. My nerves felt raw. I realized right then I was actually dying for some coffee.

"That sounds good," he agreed.

We turned and headed back up the street to the Picnic Basket. Slowly people were starting to come out to take in the damage. On the steps of the Congregational Church, Mrs. Walker, the minister's wife, was sweeping uselessly at huge fallen roof tiles and wood fragments from the steeple. Lexy Morgan and her father were bailing water out of his candy and souvenir shop. Charlie and I paused at the surreal lake of floating jawbreakers and Atomic Fireballs and offered to help. Mr. Morgan shook his head, too upset and too focused to talk. Mrs. Hilliard, my history teacher, stood in the middle of the street, staring at her car. It had been flattened under a giant maple tree, and now was an accordion of red metal and spiderwebbed glass. She looked confused, as if she'd just awakened from a dream, as if she weren't sure what she was looking at was real. I knew the feeling. I couldn't shake it.

Nobody even noticed when we entered the Picnic Basket. The stove was unlit, but Greg was toasting bagels in a toaster oven and there was a huge pot of coffee brewing, both plugged into the portable generator. Nancy was at her computer, finding out everything she could about the storm. She called out headlines to the dozen or so people huddled around her.

"No prediction of how long to restore ferry! Freak softball-sized hail across the border in New Hampshire! Coast guard expects delays of supplies and building materials to island residents in region! Lady Gaga plans Martha's Vineyard storm victim fund-raiser with Diane Sawyer and Carly Simon."

She snickered at that last one. A few others grumbled. Stone Cove Island's rivalry with Martha's Vineyard and Nantucket goes back a long way. Locals insist our island has a more low-key, discreet reputation, but a lot of people feel jealous of the glitzier image of the other two. When the president vacations in Nantucket, islanders here make a big point of saying how thankful they are for the peace and quiet of Stone Cove.

"Nancy, what about the power?" called Jim McNeil, the mechanic in town.

"Thursday at the earliest, they're saying."

That was three days from now. I could see everyone mentally calculating their supplies: water, canned food, batteries, extra blankets. So far the weather had been warm for October, but at this time of year, it could be below freezing tomorrow. I'd heard my mother worrying about that just last night, and wondering if we had enough firewood on hand. Greg looked up from his bagel station and nodded at us.

"Charlie, Eliza, you okay? Everybody good at home?"

"We're fine, Greg. Thanks," I said.

"Your dad's about to be busy, I guess. Lots of work to be done."

"Yeah, I guess it looks that way," I answered.

Charlie handed me a cup of coffee and gestured to the door. I followed him outside.

"That's about the worst way I can think of to find out what's really going on. Local news sites and gossip magazines. Let's go over to the *Gazette* and see if Jay will let us look at their wire service. Even just their Twitter feed would be better info than this."

Jay Norsworthy was the editor of our local paper, the *Stone Cove Island Gazette*—an island fixture. Charlie had interned for Jay at least one summer, and I could tell how happy Jay was to see him the second we walked in the door.

It was chaos in the tiny office. Jay was racing between his computer and the AP wire printout. His only companion was his black Lab, Sparkler. The *Gazette* had its own generator, and Jay had gotten their Internet connection half working, but there were no landlines up anywhere on the island. For a dizzying, manic moment, I felt a wave of relief. It was amazing that Jay was still managing to get the paper out on schedule, by himself, despite everything that was going on that morning. Maybe things weren't as bad as they seemed.

"Charlie, I could really use your help with the Wi-Fi. It's been on and off, creeping like a snail when it does work. Maybe you can work your magic."

"I can try." Charlie pulled the latest printout from the wire and handed it to Jay, then passed me his coffee and stooped down to take a look.

"Jay, is your house okay?" I asked. Jay lived in a cottage near the west bluffs; there was worry about erosion out there even in an ordinary storm.

"Slept here," he answered, his eyes still on the computer screen. "I knew I'd have to get the paper out early today once I saw what we were in store for last night. I hope it's still standing. It might be halfway to Rockport by now though." He laughed, but I didn't hear any humor in his voice. Here he was trying to jury-rig his Internet connection to get the town paper out and he didn't know if he still had a place to live.

Unconsciously my gaze went to Charlie. We exchanged a look. No one, I realized, really knew how bad things were yet. We would only find out by degree. My relief faded, leaving a dark hole in its place. What if people had died?

"Was anyone . . ." I hesitated, then choked out my

question. "How soon will we know if anyone is missing?" I wasn't sure how to put this.

Jay's expression was grim. "No one has been reported missing yet, as far as I've heard. But everyone's still taking stock. We should know more this afternoon. The churches are setting up check-in stations with hot food and drinks— the ones with propane stoves that can *make* hot food, anyway—and there's an evacuation center at the high school. They said only about fifteen people stayed there last night, but I've heard lots more are moving over this morning, the ones that can't stay in their homes."

"Do we know how many?" asked Charlie. He was squinting at the tiny copper pins in the USB ports, his fingers working to reattach the haphazard wiring in the block of drives and modems.

"Not yet. That's my next stop."

"This thing is flaky," Charlie complained. "Even on a good day."

"Don't I know it," muttered Jay.

Suddenly I felt the full weight of how powerless I was. Sparkler padded up to me, eyeing me as if I might have brought kibble as well as coffee. It seemed crazy that we were inside, reading reports off the wire service about what was happening to us, right now, right outside. I wanted to get back out and *do* something, anything, so I wouldn't feel so useless.

I peered over Charlie's shoulder at some more papers piled on top of the modem. The text confirmed what Nancy had told us: no power for up to a week, no ferry service for the foreseeable future, possibly until the spring depending on how fast federal emergency money would come in to repair the harbor. Someone would have to work with the coast guard to figure out how we would get food shipped in, garbage shipped out, and how people would get on and off the island. There were many more questions than answers, and all of them needed to be solved before winter set in. I was scared, thinking about how bad things could get once the temperatures really dropped. You couldn't survive on Stone Cove without heat, gasoline or a way to get food.

"If there's no ferry until spring, my dad is going to completely lose his mind," said Charlie with a grim smile.

Or starve, I thought.

He gave up trying to fix the connection and stood, taking his coffee cup back. It was no longer steaming. "Sorry, Jay."

"No worries. Your parents have been down here, you know that? It sounds like the inn did okay. They have power, at least."

Charlie sighed. "The boiler room was flooded. They are dealing with some unhappy folks."

Jay nodded. I could see his newsman's antenna sussing out a story in this last comment, a piece about those stranded, late-season guests who refused to leave despite dire warnings—island dilettantes now stuck here with the rest of us.

"I'll bet. I'll swing by later and see if I can find some way to help with that. Coast guard is holding a press conference at eleven to talk about initial transportation plans. That should be on the agenda too." He looked up at us and I noticed for the first time the dark circles ringing his eyes. "You two go and be with your families. I'll manage here."

TWO

Charlie walked me home. I couldn't help thinking that under any other circumstances, that event would have made prime Stone Cove gossip. *What is Charlie Pender doing with Eliza Elliot?* But today there was no such thing as "bizarre." Today everything was bizarre. Besides, there was no one around to whisper about or watch us; we were all alone. I kept looking for people. What was everyone doing right now, our friends and neighbors? The ruined streets were eerie and deserted, no signs of life behind the dark windows. I reminded myself there was no power. That my own mom was too afraid to go out. They must be inside, trying to stay warm, figuring out how to face the devastation.

Our house sat part of the way up the hill, still within the village. From there it was another ten-to-fifteen-minute walk up to the inn. Most guests took advantage of the inn's loaner bicycles to get back and forth to town, or a couple of golf carts the inn made available.

"It's always weird to be back," said Charlie out of nowhere.

I almost jumped. "Yeah," I said.

"This place is always so its own world. But today . . ."

"Today it's like being on another planet," I finished. "What's Jay going to do if his house is gone?"

Charlie shook his head. I pictured Jay and Sparkler moving into the *Gazette* offices permanently, making coffee on the hot plate and eating ramen noodles every night.

"Can we swing by Meredith's? Do you mind? I just want to make sure she's okay."

I'd said "we" without thinking. But it did feel like we were in this together, tossed into the same hole that we'd now have to crawl our way out of. I suppose you picture getting through a disaster with your closest friends and family, but instead you're thrown into random situations with people you would never expect. There was no question of making plans.

"Sure," said Charlie. He didn't seem to be in a rush. The problems were too big; you couldn't go straight at them. Addressing them would mean chipping away over a very long time. It made me itchy though. I wanted to jump in, start, figure out some way to put things back, fix it *now*.

I hurried ahead. Meredith would get it. Meredith, my best friend since we were toddlers, lived nearby in one of the Rose Cottages: a tourist-friendly neighborhood of really old, tiny houses—all adorned with roses trellised up the sides and over the roofs. Stone Cove Island is famous for these. People buy mugs and T-shirts decorated with pictures of Meredith's house. That was usually something we laughed about, but today I didn't feel like laughing.

Trees were scattered over her street like Pick-up Sticks.

But Meredith's house had been spared, mostly. The beautiful roses, which normally cascaded over the roof, had been torn away and were sticking up wildly, in a thorny Mohawk. The last blooms, which had lingered in the warm fall weather, were gone and so were all the leaves. The trellis was broken and dangling. It looked like a punk rock skeleton, not a tourist attraction.

"Phew. I guess they're okay." The house was standing, roof and windows intact.

Charlie trudged up behind me and nodded, his eyes far away.

When I ran to the door and knocked, nobody answered, but I could see through the taped-up windows that the inside looked relatively undisturbed as well.

"Maybe they're out getting provisions?" Charlie suggested.

"Or helping out at school." Meredith's parents taught music and art. Her mom was my favorite teacher. If they were running a storm shelter there, the whole family was likely pitching in. That antsy feeling came back. If I didn't join them, do *something*, I'd lose my mind.

TEN MINUTES LATER, WE stood side by side at the end of my pebble drive. Our house, cottage-sized by anyone's estimation, looked like a dollhouse under the massive oak.

"That is a seriously big tree," said Charlie. "You guys are lucky it only landed on the porch."

"I know. I don't think Salty is ever coming back out of my parents' closet." Salty was our ten-year-old schnauzer. He had taken cover at the first cracks of thunder last night and, last I'd checked, was still huddled in the dark with my mom's shoes.

My dad appeared from behind the trunk, sweaty under his bundled clothing and holding a chain saw. He waved hello but didn't come over. I didn't invite Charlie in.

"You okay?" Charlie asked quietly. He was looking at me now. It seemed like he could see me sinking into myself. I suppose I stared back. For the first time, I really registered the gold-flecked warmth of his brown eyes. Meredith had always harped on how Charlie had such great eyes.

"Yeah. I'm fine," I said, trying to rally. I thought of the time a few years earlier when Salty got lost on the golf course. Charlie had been nice then too, waiting with me on the steps of the inn while my dad walked up and down the links with a flashlight, calling Salty's name and shaking a bag of treats. Of course Salty eventually trotted out of the brush, covered in burrs and something stinky, acting like nothing had happened.

"I'll see you around, okay?" he said. "Stay safe."

"You too," I said. After one more glance at our house, he hurried away. I wasn't anxious to head inside. Just the thought made me a little claustrophobic. I wondered if my dad would let me try the chain saw. Honestly, it looked kind of fun. I stepped toward him.

"Forget it," my dad said, following my eyes and pursing his lips. "Go help your mom dry out stuff inside."

I smirked, and to prove I could handle a chain saw, showed off my tree-trunk-climbing technique, landing with a thud near the front door.

"Nice," he said. "Next time try going through the back.

You're going to take down the porch completely if the tree doesn't get it done first."

"What? You fixed the door? Maybe I should check your temperature. You're clearly delirious."

"Ha-ha. Hilarious, missy." He reached for the chain saw cord, then paused. "Wait, tell me about things in town."

My smile faded. "It's bad," I said. "Ferry's out for at least a couple of months. Plus, no power and no phone lines, obviously."

"Damn. We knew it could happen, but I guess we never believed it."

"But we'll fix it, right?" I knew I sounded like a little girl, but I couldn't help myself.

"Of course, kiddo. This island's seen worse."

I wasn't sure that was true, but it made me feel better to hear him say it.

Inside, Mom had stripped the wet sheets off my bed and was hanging them to dry in the bathroom. She had rolled up the rugs from the first floor and dragged them to the back door. We had a small generator and a camp stove that ran on Sterno, but the generator was not going to power the clothes dryer. She looked up as I came into the bathroom, her forehead lined with stress, her blonde hair in a mess of a bun. Her lips were pinched in a tight smile that wasn't fooling anyone, especially me. It was an expression I'd seen often. I tried to picture her at my age. Her hair was pretty and silky, more golden than mine. She was tall and slender, but so much tension and fatigue radiated from her body.

"Oh, good, Eliza, you can help me. Hold this up while I grab the other side."

"Mom, why don't we hang them outside?"

"What if it rains? Or if there's another storm?"

"There is not going to be another storm like this. Hurricane season is almost over. This stuff'll never dry in here. It'll stay damp and the house will stay damp." I could see the new worry of toxic mold fluttering behind her eyes. She had never been seventeen, I decided. It was impossible to imagine her having one beer too many at a beach party, giggling on a bike ride with friends or daydreaming over a crush, her marriage to my dad notwithstanding. I turned on the sink faucet to wash my hands.

"Don't touch that!" she yelped. I jumped back and banged my head on the medicine cabinet door, which was open.

"Why?"

"It might be contaminated. We don't know if the water is safe. You're supposed to boil it—"

"Mom. I'm just washing my hands. I'm not drinking it. Stop freaking out." I left the room without helping with the sheets. I felt bad, but I just couldn't take it. Wasn't she supposed to be calming me down? *I* was the kid, not her. She was so exhausting.

I lay down on my stripped bed. The edge of the mattress felt wet. I stared at the ceiling, the only part of my room that looked unchanged. My rug was gone. My dresser had been dragged to the middle of the floor. The pictures on the wall along the window were ruined. There were brown, rusty stripes running down the walls where the roof had leaked through the ceiling and under the paint. My entire last semester of life drawing had melted into a leaden, gooey, newsprint brick in the corner.

My mom hadn't even asked about my trip to town. The whole place could have washed away and she hadn't given it a second thought. Her self-absorption was insane. I was not going to be like her. I was going to pitch in and do something—in fact, I would organize something. Something big. Our house was fine. We could survive with a little water and having to use the back door. Other people had bigger problems, and I was going to focus on the future of the island, not my mother's petty neuroses. I got back up and headed out the newly operational back door to climb the hill to the Anchor Inn.

Before I had time to reach the top of the steps to the inn's service entrance, Charlie opened the door.

"Oh, hey," he said, looking surprised. "What are you doing here?"

THREE

Jay at the *Gazette* came through. On cleanup day, we had twenty-four kids from the high school including me, six from the middle school, a handful of volunteer parents and Officer Bailey, our town sheriff, who offered to organize transportation and garbage removal.

Granted, there had been some awkward weirdness in organizing the whole thing. Colleen Guinness, local lacrosse star and part-time waitress at the Anchor Inn, wanted to know why I'd come up to see Charlie that morning after the storm. She wasn't mean about it, and a part of me was just relieved that she had shown up to work that day. Besides, if she were curious about my motives for seeing Charlie, it meant that Stone Cove Island was still itself: small, familial, and gossipy.

My memory of the conversation with Charlie had blurred over the three days, but I thought it consisted mostly of me rambling. "I want to organize a cleanup day. Kids from the high school. Younger kids, too. The island will be ours eventually, right? Shouldn't we be the ones to help rebuild it? So I was thinking if you talked to Jay, and if Jay put it in the *Gazette*, people would show up. I really feel like it's the only way to get through this: get outside your head and your own problems and help someone else. If we sit home feeling miserable about what's happened to us, we'll just be stuck. We have to all pitch in if we want things to go back to the way they were . . ."

Charlie had interrupted me there. "Listen, Eliza. You love it here. I get that. I love it too in lots of ways. I just think that one way people keep everything so perfect, the same way it's been for two hundred years—"

"Two hundred and fifty years," I corrected. It was obnoxious. I knew that. It just came out.

"Yes, excuse me, Miss Island History. *For two hundred and forty-seven years*, is by keeping out any new ideas."

"My cleanup crew is a new idea," I pointed out.

"Not what I meant. But yes, I'll help. You want some more coffee? I'm going to get a refill. We should drink the good stuff while we can, because I have a feeling we're in for months of FEMA coffee."

Standing there with Colleen—my not-quite-friend but Stone Cove sister and survivor—I could imagine soon, without regular food shipments, coffee would come to stand in for gold. Through the window, I watched guys in white jumpsuits from FEMA unload supplies from the driveway up to the inn kitchen. Fast work. They must have come in by helicopter. I was certain that Charlie was wrong. The reason the island was able to preserve its way of life was because everyone here shared a common vision of how they wanted to live. Not because anyone was telling anyone else what to do.

At least I thought so then.

THE DAY ITSELF WAS not the crisp, sunny autumn day I had pictured. It was humid, weirdly warm and raining on and off. There was hardly any wind. Harney's hardware had donated work gloves. I put on jeans, rain boots and a windbreaker and took off on my bike at dawn. For three days I had felt trapped and helpless, fixated on the state of Stone Cove and wondering how we would ever be able to rebuild it. The good news was nobody had died. An older lady from the bluffs was initially unaccounted for, but it turned out she had evacuated to her sister's house in Salem, just like she was supposed to. Two ten-year-old boys were feared drowned. Really, they had decided to camp out in the light-house during the storm, and then were afraid to go home the next day and find out how much trouble they were in.

I met Meredith at the Little Kids' Park. She was already waiting, straddling her bike, dressed from top to bottom in foul-weather gear. Despite the many years of lessons we'd taken together, I was the one who ended up the big sailor. She hated cold water and soggy shoes. I was surprised she still even had that old slicker. Meredith was a dancer. She had started ballet at six and had stayed serious about it ever since. We made friends instantly in that first class our moms had signed us up for. I'd only lasted about six weeks. It was too slow and I was too fidgety. I had thought dancing would mean, well, dancing, not standing still, holding onto a bar and bending your knees.

We called Putney Park the Little Kids' Park because it's where our parents used to take us when we were in nursery school. Only a few trees remained standing. The playground, which sat in a low spot in the center, was completely flooded. The baby swings hovered over a deep pool of brown water that stopped a few inches below the rubber tire seats. The little slide was half submerged. Crews were working on clearing streets and damaged buildings first, so the parks and beaches had to wait.

"Ready?" Meredith asked, her eyes bright. Despite being a devout herbal tea drinker, she always looked way more awake than I felt.

"Storm's over," I joked, giving her outfit a once-over. Meredith rolled her eyes. "My mom made me change out of my regular raincoat. She didn't want me to get it dirty. It was this or one of her painting smocks."

"Well, we'll probably be inside mostly. We're on light-house duty."

THE FANCIEST HOUSES ON the island sat along the bluff on the west side, just north of Jay Norsworthy's (luckily still inhabitable) house. Normally the bluff was fairly protected from wind because it faced the mainland, but I had heard some summer people were now rethinking that location. The cliff had been eroding slowly for years, and the hurricane had speeded the process. A few houses would either need to be braced on pilings and tied into the hillside or end up in the ocean.

There were also rambling, huge, old-fashioned summer houses out on East Beach, past the lighthouse. I loved that part of the island. The houses there felt gracious, stretching out into the surrounding open fields. Some kept horses or cows. Few were occupied by year-rounders though, unless they were caretakers. We tended to live in the central section of town just up the hill from Water Street—my neighborhood—or else up behind the inn, or down in the little row houses along the harbor. A few people lived near the marina off East Beach, but in the winter, you really wanted to be close to town. People farther out could get snowed in for days.

As we rode, I tried not to take in the flattened trees, half-collapsed houses and sad debris washed from people's basements: endless sodden photo albums, ruined toys, lost sports trophies, mud-encrusted kids' snowsuits. On the steep hill down from the harbor, we passed the road sign that said DO NOT COAST. We coasted, letting our bikes fly, no brakes until we neared the bottom, and the bikes were rattling so hard our bones shook. The wind pulled at the skin on our faces. I looked over at Meredith. She was grinning like I was. We did this every time, without thinking. We had always done this. When we were kids, we would take our hands off the handlebars.

"What did your mom say about school?" I asked her. They were trying to decide when to open again. The building wasn't damaged, but they were still using the gym as temporary housing and weren't sure if they could operate the whole building off generators alone.

"Next week," she said. "Tuesday. Wednesday at the latest."

I wrinkled my nose, the wind whipping through my hair.

I was getting used to having free time and I liked it. Meredith and others, who were more worried than I was about college admission tests and applications, were anxious for the high school to open. Meredith wanted to get into Barnard, where there was a really good dance program.

We distracted ourselves talking about the Halloween dance, pretending that the immediate future was predictable. Meredith had a crush on Tim McAllister, a junior. She was obsessed with what people would think about her dating a younger boy. If she ever got around to dating him, that is. So far the whole thing was theoretical.

"Tim's birthday is March twenty-second," she said. "That means I am really only four months older."

"So you've pointed out at least eight billion times."

She shot a quick smirk at me as we slowed, approaching the beach. "I'm picturing what Lily Kirby and those guys would say, but it's not like I couldn't go with someone in our grade. I could. I just happen to like Tim." Meredith had worked the whole thing into a star-crossed drama in her mind, though I was pretty sure Tim would be thrilled to go to the party with her if he had any clue she even liked him.

"You know what I think," I said. "Just ask him."

"Who are you going to go with?" she asked.

"I don't know," I said. "Maybe Josh again. Or maybe I won't go with anyone." Josh and I had had a thing for about a second last year before deciding that we were better as friends, which we still were. My mind flitted to Charlie. But Charlie wouldn't be here by then, and could anything be lamer than going to a dance at the school you just graduated from? "We should just go as a group again. Do a theme costume. The seven deadly sins or something."

"That could be fun," she said. But I could tell she was still thinking about Tim.

As we dismounted and ditched our bikes, I took in the long expanse of sand. Yes, it was littered with garbage, broken branches and broken bits of dock, but it was still there, still recognizable as East Beach. I took a big stack of heavy-gauge garbage bags from Officer Bailey. Meredith kept her distance. Most kids did when it came to our chief local law enforcement official. She was a stocky woman about my mom's age, built very straight up and down. She wore her uniform's belt buckled in tight, but didn't really have a waist. Officer Bailey was the first woman sheriff in the island's history, and the jokes and rumors flew: she was really a man; she was a closet lesbian; she couldn't get a job off the island on a "real" police force because of her weight. Personally, I thought it was cool that she was the first female sheriff of Stone Cove Island, even if she had zero social skills.

Some of the boys were dragging garbage cans onto the beach where kids had started stacking wood and raking up debris.

Colleen was among them. She held up a bright green, high-heeled shoe she'd dug out of the sand.

"It's my size! Maybe I'll find the other one."

I laughed, but was also thinking it would be a good idea to come up with some way to connect people with their lost belongings, maybe start a website where people could post pictures. I could put that together. I would need someone more tech savvy than I was. Once again, my mind flitted to

Charlie. *He's going back to Boston,* I reminded myself. *And you already asked your favor. Leave the guy alone.*

"Thanks for coming!" I called.

"No worries," Colleen yelled back. "It's a great idea!"

Meredith and I handed out extra work gloves and then went into the lighthouse carrying rakes and shovels. The tall tower was painted outside and in with wide black and white stripes all the way up to the lantern room. It had been in operation until the early nineties, marking the channel that led back to the marina. Park rangers checked in on their rounds, but mostly it sat empty, open to tourists who wanted to climb up and take in the view.

That wasn't a possibility now. Standing water and soaked papers and cardboard carpeted the floor. We winced at the odor: dank, stale mildew. Sand had blown inside and formed a mini dune against the far wall. Meredith and I hung garbage bags off the metal stair railing and began to fill them with the rotten paper. We moved shovelful after shovelful of sand back outside where it belonged. The wet sand was heavy. After ten minutes, my T-shirt was dripping. I tied a bandanna over my hair, hippie style, to keep the sweat off my face. After a while Colleen joined us.

"I came in here thinking this job would be easier," she said, struggling with the sand.

"Ha!" I grunted. Meredith just shook her head.

"You got a good turnout, Eliza," Colleen said.

"I'm just happy people actually showed up." It was funny how in the last few days Colleen had come to feel like a friend. Before the storm I couldn't remember more than two times we'd said anything other than hello. "Hey, did you happen to see Charlie this morning? He's still here on the island, right? Do you know if he's coming out to help?"

It came out before I really thought. She shot me a huge grin.

"Not a joiner. I told you," said Colleen. "Seriously. You two are ridiculous. He's about to leave. What are you wasting time for?"

"You and Charlie?" Meredith piled on. "Why didn't you tell me you hooked up?"

"Because we didn't. He helped me with cleanup day; you know, by getting Jim to put it in the *Gazette*. I want to thank him. That's all."

"You should invite him to Halloween," said Meredith.

Colleen rolled her eyes. "You snooze you lose, Eliza."

"There's nothing *to* lose," I groaned. But I could feel myself blushing. It was true, I had been looking around the beach for Charlie, feeling disappointed—okay, even annoyed—that he hadn't shown up. But this wasn't about me. We were doing this for the island. It wasn't like he hadn't shown up to my birthday party or something. "I'm going to check the windows upstairs," I announced, even though I knew they were fine. I could see from outside they weren't broken.

As I climbed the spiral staircase, away from the pesky questions, the air became fresher. I could taste the tang of salt. The view was still as beautiful as ever. The ocean was calm, rolling in leisurely, innocently, as though nothing had happened. On the upper landing, a narrow stairway led to the observation deck. To the left there was a door, normally locked, the former office of the lighthouse keeper. Now it sat halfway open, blown in from the force of the storm. I pushed my way into the office and sighed.

The place looked like that illustration in *Alice in Wonderland*, the one where she's standing in a mad swirl of playing cards. The papers—seemingly every scrap from the entire lifespan of the place—were plastered across all available surfaces. It looked like a bomb had exploded. It would take a week of cleanup days to put this right.

"Wow." I think I actually said it out loud. There was almost no water damage up here, and I couldn't figure out how the storm had created a little tornado in here without tearing out the windows in the process. I reached down and picked up something at my feet.

It was a letter.

It had been written on a typewriter, not printed from a computer. The paper was heavy stationery, the formal blue kind people use for thank-you notes. This was no thank-you note.

Uninvited guest. There's no room here for you. Daddy is waiting at the bottom of the sea. Square peg. Break your mother's back. We make the rules. You had your chance to play.

Do not await the last judgment. It takes place every day. To breathe is to judge. Eleven, twelve, dig and delve. Anchor through your throat. Down came a blackbird and pecked off her nose.

Good-bye, Bess. Read this out loud so you can hear your name one more time. You didn't have to go but now you will. Don't say no one warned you.

FOUR

After I read the letter a second time, I realized I wasn't breathing. What was this? There was no date. The paper was damp, as though it had been sitting out for a long time, but every piece of paper on the island was probably damp at this point. I recognized the bits of nursery rhyme, of course, but parts of it sounded biblical: "Do not await the last judgment." What kind of person had written this thing?

My first thought was that I should show it to Officer Bailey. But it was so hard to tell if it meant anything. It was creepy, definitely, but it could have easily just been the start of someone's short story for creative writing class. Officer Bailey would think I was overreacting. I almost certainly was overreacting. I folded it and put it in the pocket of my windbreaker. I closed the office door behind me and went down to help finish cleaning up the lower floor.

For the rest of the afternoon, I felt cold and couldn't warm up. I didn't show Meredith. I still don't know why. Instead I took the letter home.

MY BED WAS STILL stripped. The rug hung outside, drying. My mother had conceded one point to the side of rationality. The sun was already low in the afternoon sky.

I'd been sitting on my floor for almost an hour, rereading the letter over and over. I thought about my parents and their constant reminders: *You can talk to us about anything. We are here if you need us. Any problem you have, bring it to us.* Platitudes every teenage girl hears.

Normally I thought of myself as pretty self-sufficient. But I didn't know what to do with this. This time, I *did* want their help, but I didn't know how to ask. So I sat there, waiting for it to be time for dinner. And when my dad finally yelled for me to come down, I brought the letter with me.

"How was cleanup day?" he asked as we gathered around the kitchen table.

"Good. Really good," I said. "Look. I found this in the lighthouse." I thrust the paper at him. I couldn't beat around the bush when I didn't even understand what I was showing them.

My dad's eyes met Mom's as he took the blue sheet. He had a crescent-shaped scar on his left hand; a hammer had fallen at a construction site during one of his first summer construction jobs in high school. It seemed to quiver as he read the page. I glanced up and saw his eyes zigzag, zigzag and stop. He sat frozen—so frozen that when my mom plucked it from his hand, he didn't stop her. My mom's eyes only completed the zig of the first line and without zagging, she was up, crying, arms flailing and tearing from the room.

I was used to my mom's histrionics. But frankly, this scared me. My dad was looking at me in a fixed, parental, trying-to-be-calm-but-I-have-no-idea-what-to-do expression. Finally he spoke. First he said, "Eliza. It's okay. You didn't do anything wrong." There was a long pause as he figured out his next move.

"It happened when we were in high school," he began again, once he seemed to have decided on a route. "Your mom had a best friend—we were all friends with this girl Bess. She was a great girl. Difficult family life though. Our senior year, Bess drowned at East Beach. Now, I don't want to scare you, but at the time, it seemed likely that she was killed." He waited, checking in to see that I was still with him. I was.

"Willa—your mom—never really got over this. It's something that upsets her a lot to think about. It took a long time before she could get past it."

"Why have I never heard about this?" I asked. Poor Mom. If anyone was not cut out to survive her best friend's murder, it was Willa Elliot. I felt a momentary softening of my perennial frustration.

"Well, to be honest, the whole island had a hard time getting over it. Not only was it terrible to lose this young girl that everybody loved, but it brought so much bad publicity and pressure. You know what it's like here, Eliza. So many people survive only on the island's success as a tourist destination. The pain about the murder, and the gossip and fear about whether the island would survive the bad press—it split people apart and it's still . . . I know twenty-five years is more than a lifetime to you, but people still really do not like to think about it."

"So, you think this is a letter from her killer?" The question popped out of my mouth before I'd even fully formed the thought.

"No." Dad gave me a patient smile. "No, I definitely don't think that. Who even knows when it was written? I bet it was someone with an active imagination, somebody who knows the island lore and was bored. I think it's absolutely nothing. Really." He handed it back to me, to show he was done thinking about it.

"Dad," I said. "What happened to her?"

For a moment, he almost looked like he might tell me. Then he said, "Please don't bring this up with your mother. It was so hard for her the first time losing Bess. I don't want her to have to go through it again."

"Okay," I said. What else can you say when your dad asks you something like that?

THAT NIGHT, I LAY in my sleeping bag on the still-dry edge of my bed. I could hear my parents through the wall in the next room. My mom was crying, half wailing and half whining. It was hard to make out her words.

"Nate. It's my fault. You know it's my fault," was what I thought I heard.

But it didn't sound like my dad was comforting my mom. He sounded angry. "God damn it Willa!" he shouted. His voice had no trouble penetrating the wall. "I will not go through this again. She is gone. You want to do this again, you do it by yourself."

THE NEXT DAY WAS sunny, crisp, and beautiful, as though the storm had never happened. I woke up early and lay for a long time, listening to the birds chirp outside my window. All night I had been in a half-sleep limbo, and now I was both exhausted and wide awake. It was pointless to stay in bed. I took a quick shower and dressed, feeling jittery. A short, bleary bike ride later I was at the Picnic Basket, buying coffee and a pumpkin muffin and listening to Nancy lecture on the differences between the FEMA of hurricane Katrina and the FEMA of now, and how Congress better not get in the way of us getting the disaster relief we needed before next summer.

I thought of asking Nancy what she remembered about Bess and the murder. But then I thought of my dad, his angry tone last night, and what he had said about people's reluctance to talk. I decided I was better off finding out as much as I could on my own first. I could feel myself starting to obsess, but I couldn't help it. My mother had a secret she'd never shared. Her best friend had been murdered, and she had never even mentioned it. It was so spooky, as though the ghost of this girl no one wanted to remember had been walking the island all these years, and only now I could feel her presence. People really did know how to keep their mouths shut around here. But at what cost? Was that why my mom was such a high-strung ball of nerves, even before Hurricane Victor?

I imagined Meredith murdered and wondered, *Would*

I ever get over that? My life would be ripped apart. Would I talk about it? Or would I pretend it never happened? I was pretty sure I would talk about it, but you never really knew what you would do in extreme situations until those situations sought you out.

I had only two pieces of information to go on: it was an infamous murder that took place on the island (how many could there be?), and the dead girl's name was Bess.

At the library, I was briefly stymied by the fact that the Internet connection had not been restored, though the power had. Mary Ellen, however, the wispy, gray-haired, always-smiling librarian, was able to introduce me to the old way of storing news stories: microfiche, rolls of film you unspooled on a light table in a headache-inducing blur. If you wanted August of 1990, for example, you had to let every section of the whole daily paper zip past you to find the one relevant story you were looking for. Mary Ellen seemed thrilled that somebody was actually willing to put in the time to do research the old-fashioned way. How did people survive without search engines?

Two hours later, I had found eight stories on Bess Linsky, but there were many more I hadn't yet unfurled. Unlike Google, I had to read through each one before I could figure out if it was relevant. Each story ran a version in some varying size of her school photo. Her hair was shaggy, chin-length and brown. Her eyes were large and open, with thick lashes, their expression kind. For some reason she reminded me of a doe, surprised in the woods. Her nose turned up and had a dust of freckles across it. She was smiling. She had no idea what was going to happen to her.

She was so pretty, I thought, and she looked so friendly. Or was that just what we projected onto a photograph of someone we knew was dead? Eventually I shut my eyes and pushed aside the microfiche rolls. I couldn't look at that picture anymore without conjuring the rest of her life. I saw her walking home from school with my mom, eating late-night fries in the diner—maybe sailing the same Mercury sailboat I'd learned on at camp, helping her dad hose down rental boats in the marina.

I felt seasick. I needed fresh air.

On the steps out front, I found Charlie Pender. He greeted me with that warm, unguarded smile of his. But he looked as if he hadn't slept or even changed his jeans. Circles ringed his bleary brown eyes. His hair was rumpled. Things must have been worse at the inn than I'd realized.

"Oh, hi," I said, a little surprised to see him, though I wasn't even sure how he would have gotten off the island at this point. "You're still here." It sounded like a question, or worse, an accusation, which was the last thing I intended.

"Yeah. I'm still here. Sorry I missed your big cleanup. I was trying to work things out with the *Boston Globe* all day. I told them I needed to stay, at least for a couple of weeks, to help my family get things working again."

I felt an awful swirl of happy for me and bummed for him at this news. Instead of what I meant, I muttered, "It wasn't my day. It was for the island." How did I have any friends? It was inconceivable. But Charlie was too nice to take the bait.

"It *was* your day. Look how much you put into it."

I sat down next to him. "Yeah, well, it turned out to be super weird. I wish you had been there."

"Why?" he asked. "What happened?"

I explained about finding the letter and my parents' reaction. Then I showed it to him.

His eyes lingered over the blue paper for several minutes. He chewed his lip, his brow furrowed. I found myself looking at his hands. They were rough and chapped, like everyone else's on the island, everyone still struggling to clean up.

"Whoa," he finally breathed, handing it back to me.

"Did you ever hear anything about this?"

"No. Definitely not. Which is weird, right?"

"That's what I thought. So that's what I'm doing here." I stretched, working out the kinks in my back from having sat hunched in the same position for so long. "Scrolling through microfiche to find out what I can."

"Microfiche. Ouch. Jay made me learn how to do research on that at one point. He thought it would be good for me to know how to use it."

I managed a grin. "Awesome. Does that mean you have some leftover Dramamine you can give me?"

"Sorry." He laughed. "Just stare at the horizon until you feel better." That was an old sailing trick.

"Thanks a lot."

"Come on," he said. "I can lend another pair of eyes."

Back in the library, Charlie helped me operate the rickety system, pointing out dozens of more stories, both local and national. We tried to organize them by date. The murder had occurred on August 17, high tourist season. There were lots of Op-Ed pieces, reactions from island visitors and locals. There was also an article in the *Providence Journal* featuring a quote from Charlie's grandfather: "It's certainly tragic. I hope that they find the girl. But one accident is no reflection on the magical retreat that is Stone Cove Island."

"He started the inn," said Charlie, by way of explanation. He sounded slightly embarrassed at his grandfather's cold tone, not that I could blame him. "I'm sure it was pretty bad for business that summer."

"I would guess."

By mid-September, the story abruptly died out.

There were no more tourists around. The police had no new information. Suddenly island business owners "could not be reached for further comment" and residents "declined to be interviewed." Newspapers referred to old information and prior interviews and then seemed to give up. A girl swimming out—or being dragged out—into the ocean was unlikely ever to be found again. That made logical sense, but there was something horrible about abandoning the search for the truth so easily.

"It says they found her clothes covered in blood," I mused, stretching again. I was ready for more fresh air. "And her hair had been cut off. Couldn't they test the DNA and see if anyone else's samples showed up?" I thought about how sickening those details were. There was something about the killer removing her hair . . . such an intensely cruel and humiliating gesture.

"I don't know when they started using that in investigations exactly. We should look that up too." Charlie took out a small notebook and jotted something down.

"Do you always carry that around with you?" I asked. What I really wanted to ask was: *Why are you helping me and why are you being so nice?* But I could tell he was as disturbed and intrigued by Bess Linsky's murder as I was. The secret had been kept from him, too, and the Penders were at the top of the island's social hierarchy. Maybe his parents had their own reasons for wanting to forget.

"I never go anywhere without my notebook." He glanced up from the page. "It's weird that a huge story like this faded so fast, don't you think?"

"I was just thinking the same thing. But I guess if there's no new information, what can they say? They can only rehash the story so much."

He nodded, his tired eyes distant. "It seems really quick to just let it go a month later. It's almost like they made a decision together to stop talking."

"People were probably scared. About what happened to Bess and about what would happen the next summer if no one showed up." I could almost understand the immediate reaction better than the decades of silence that followed. Shaking off the aches, I turned back to the machine. Fresh air could wait. "Let's look at local stories from the next summer and see what happened afterward."

We scrolled through the *Gazette* as well as the papers from Gloucester, Salem, Boston, and Providence. There was almost no mention of Bess, and no stories with new information. But it was hard to tell, going through the microfiche, what we were overlooking.

"I am so missing Google right now," said Charlie. "Can I see the letter again?" We reread it together.

"What's with the nursery rhymes? It's like it's right out of an eighties serial killer movie."

"I know," I said. "And then the rest of the stuff about judgment? That feels more like a religious freak. They don't seem like the thoughts of the same person."

Charlie made another note. "We should look into serial killers from around then just in case there's something that fits, like chopping her hair off. We'll have to wait till we can get online though. It's too random, looking this way."

"We could find out more about her though. Old school newspapers? Or yearbooks?"

"Good idea. We can find out what kind of person she was, who she hung out with, what kind of activities she was into."

"Charlie, you really never heard about this? Before today?"

"No. Had you?"

"I think it's so weird. My mother was apparently best friends with her. Your parents know everything about the island. People like Nancy and Greg? Kids at school? It's like the biggest thing that's ever happened here before last week, and no one talks about it? I never thought of Stone Cove as a place with dark secrets."

Charlie rolled his eyes. "What?" I asked.

"Not you. This place. It might not be a dark secret. Maybe some kids at school do know about it. Maybe we just never happened to hear. I wonder if her mother still lives here." I noticed the way Charlie looked to the side and up slightly, through his lashes, when he was really thinking.

"We would know that. And she never spoke to reporters, so it's not likely she would be around talking about it now."

Charlie nodded. I could see he was considering the angles. "It's a good Nancy question."

"True. If anyone is going to talk . . ."

We walked to the periodical room, where one of the librarians pointed out where the yearbooks were kept. We grabbed a thin stack of them: Bess's and our parents' year, the previous year and the year after. As I sat down, I felt a prickling of the hair at the base of my neck.

"I can't believe something like this could happen here," I said. Charlie nodded. He had flipped to the section about the senior class and was scanning the pages for Bess's image.

Because Stone Cove High was small, each senior had three pages devoted to his or her school career. There was the portrait page (tense grin, eyes focused too high, swirly mauve pull-down backdrop). The next page detailed accomplishments (usually people really milked it, listing activities they'd started and quit after one meeting, or activities everyone in the class was required to do). The most important was the "collage page." This was meant to show off your personality with cool quotations (Kurt Cobain's lyrics were the most popular), demonstrate how many friends you had (either in volume or by proximity to popular kids) and immortalize great moments (*"Dudes, Lone Rock Bar '89! Never forget!"*).

Charlie flipped past shots of varsity stars, gothy loners, hippie Deadheads, mathletes and early adopters of grunge.

Because of the circumstances, the format of Bess's section was slightly different from the other seniors'. Charlie handed the book to me so I could get a better look. After the portrait page—by now I knew the doe eyes, the dust of freckles as though she was my own friend—there was a white page with a single quotation across the center:

"To live in hearts we leave behind, is not to die."—*Thomas Campbell*

The school portrait, I now realized, must have been from her junior year, since she had been killed before the senior year pictures would have been taken.

The third page of crowded candids was devoted to memories of all things Bess. Bess after a track meet, Bess in a Halloween costume dressed as Dorothy, as a toddler dressed in high-heeled shoes, and—this is the one that grabbed my full attention—Bess captured with her two best friends. Under this image, the caption read, "The three musketeers!" I almost dropped the yearbook. Charlie and I turned to stare at each other, stunned and unable to make sense of the picture. Grinning for the camera, arms flung around each other and heads pressed together in classic besties pose were three girls: Bess with both our mothers.

FIVE

Charlie and I walked home without speaking. I barely
noticed the ruined houses and rubble we passed. I was
deep inside my own thoughts, wishing I had a time-travel
machine so that I could go back twenty-five years and find
out how it was possible that my mom had once been best
friends with Cat. Best friends with Cat? Could it be that I
didn't even know my own mother? I certainly didn't understand her, but that was hardly breaking news. Charlie was
equally preoccupied. He was paying attention enough to
grab my shoulder just in time to prevent me from falling
into a hole where the paving had caved in, but otherwise
he didn't say a word.

When we got to my house, we stood a moment, looking
at each other, and then he gave me a wry, half grin and
said, "So. We'll talk more I guess."

"Uh, yeah," I said. "It looks like there might be a lot
more to talk about."

"Are you going to ask your mom about it?"

"My dad already warned me off bringing it up. She's . . .

fragile, I guess is the nice way to put it. She can't take too much stress. She gets really overwhelmed." Charlie nodded. I couldn't tell if he was being sympathetic or if he was nodding because he and everyone else on the island already knew what a mess my mom was. "So I can't mention Bess. But I could ask about your mom. When my dad's not there?"

"There's no way my mom would tell me the truth," said Charlie. "But I'm still going to ask her. We can compare notes tomorrow, if you want. Diner, nine A.M.?"

"Do they have power?" I asked.

"They have a generator. I was there the other day. They at least have coffee and, I don't know, maybe dry cereal?"

"That sounds delicious. Can we make it ten?"

"We can make it any time you say, Eliza."

I smiled yes. It suddenly seemed we had a—I didn't know what to call it, a project?—together. It felt more like it had reached out and grabbed us than that we had chosen it. But we were in it, whether it had a hold of us or we had a hold of it, and I somehow had the feeling neither side was going to let go.

After dinner, I waited for my dad to retreat to his workshop in the shed. I offered to help with the dishes. My mom and I stood side by side at the kitchen counter while she dipped the plates in the soapy water and rubbed them until they made annoying squeaks. Then she handed them to me, dripping too-hot water onto my sleeves. We had a dishwasher, but there were a lot of things my mom refused to run through it, afraid they would be ruined. It was easier to talk like this, side by side, instead of facing each other.

"I ran into Charlie Pender at the library today," I began. "Oh," she said. "He's still here? Didn't he graduate?"

"He was visiting. I don't think he has a lot of choice about staying for now. Unless he has a friend with a helicopter." My mom shrugged, like she had no idea, but if I said so she guessed it must be true. "You were in the same class as his mom, right? In high school?"

I heard the back door, my dad coming, stomping mud off his feet. I was about to be out of time, but I'd already broached the topic. It would seem weird if I brought it up again later. Mom would wonder why I was suddenly so interested in Cat Pender. So I pressed on, deciding I would make it quick before he came in.

"Were you guys friends? Did you hang out much?"

"It was so long ago, I don't really remember. We were never that close."

"No?" I asked. *Three musketeers!* I thought, seeing the caption in my head. "So you didn't really know her? It's such a small school. I mean, it was even smaller back then, wasn't it?"

She turned to look at me, but when I met her eyes she seemed to be looking through me. *Haunted* was the word that came to mind. At the same moment, my dad walked in. He looked at my mom, took in her state of mind instantly and said, "Eliza, shouldn't you be getting ready for school tomorrow?"

It came out rushed and harsh. I opened my mouth to answer at the same time he remembered. "Oh. Not till Tuesday. Right. Well, I'll finish up here." It was Saturday. I wouldn't have had school anyway.

"Willa?" he asked. "We almost done here?" My mom nodded and didn't say anything more. I went to my room.

Around eleven, my dad poked his head in to check on me and say good night. I was under my quilt, reading *Into the Wild*, dressed in the long underwear I usually used for skiing. Without any heat, the house was cold and damp. Salty lay at the foot of my bed, hogging the covers. He had agreed to come out of hiding, but was still on high alert for any reason to retreat to Mom's closet.

"Eliza. You know I asked you not to bring up Bess with your mom." He had his disappointed dad voice on.

"Dad, I didn't." He looked like he didn't believe me. He was waiting for me to say more.

"I asked her about Cat. You know I've been hanging out with Charlie Pender a little this week?"

"Yeah." He smiled slightly. "I had kinda noticed that."

"So, I just realized his mom and Mom were probably in the same class. I mean, your class. I was just asking Mom if she'd known her in high school." It was a lie, but a very white one.

"If she'd known her?" The way he said it emphasized the silliness of the question. There had probably been less than forty people in their class.

"Well, obviously she knew her," I said. "I just wondered, I don't know, whether they were friends, what Cat was like. She's intimidating, don't you think? Kind of hard to figure out."

"Yeah," he agreed. "Next time ask me. I was in the same class. I'll tell you anything you want to know."

"Okay," I said.

"Good night, kiddo." He started to close my door.

"Wait!" I called. "You didn't answer my question. So, what was Cat like? Were they friends? Was she different in high school?"

He came back into the room, but looked like he didn't want to.

"Yeah, they were—well, there was a whole gang of kids, you know, with your mom, and that girl Bess. Cat was part of it. A whole crowd of people. I can't really remember who was close with whom. It probably switched around a lot. You're in high school. You know how that goes."

"Uh-huh." I didn't. I'd had one best friend since first grade. "You were friends with Bess?"

"Yeah." His expression softened, remembering. "She was such a smart, funny girl. She had a hard time. She and her mom weren't really from here. I don't think Bess ever felt like she fit in. And she liked to argue. If she had her own idea about something, she wanted you to hear her out, to the end. Other kids took that the wrong way sometimes. Thought she was pushy, where she was just up for a good debate. She was a great friend for your mom that way, always made Willa stand up for herself. It was a terrible thing. Really, one of the most terrible things I've been through, including September eleventh."

"What was Mom like?" I asked. More than anything, I wanted him to keep going.

He laughed, a wry laugh that sounded more like a harsh exhale. "I don't know, Eliza. The same. People don't change that much. You, for example, are exactly the same impulsive, impatient little Tasmanian devil you were as a toddler."

"Thanks," I said. He was a skilled subject changer.

"Tasmanian devil in the best sense of the word, of course."

"Of course," I agreed. "And that's two words."

"Oh, hey," he said, like it was an afterthought. "One more thing. Can I have that letter you found?"

"You said you thought it was nothing."

"I do think it's nothing. But I still think we should give it to Officer Bailey, so she can be the one to decide it's nothing."

"Okay," I said. "I almost gave it to her that day I found it at the lighthouse. But I thought she might laugh at me."

"Well," he said. "Now she can laugh at me. But I wouldn't want either of us to get in trouble if it did turn out to be something. You know?"

"Yeah. That makes sense." I hesitated. "Dad, do you mind if I find it in the morning for you? It's in my back-pack with all my books for school. I have to dig it out of a pile of stuff."

"Yeah. No problem. You get some sleep." He blew a kiss from across the room, then clicked off the hall light before shutting my door and padding away down the hall. I liked it that I had the kind of dad who could install a sink or break up an old driveway, but would also blow kisses good night or rub your feet if they hurt after ice-skating. After he was gone, I switched on the reading light by my bed and pulled my math notebook out of my bag. The letter was in the drawer of my nightstand, right on top. I took a pen and started to copy it down on a square-ruled inner page of my calculus book.

"HOW CAN A SIMPLE, innocent question like 'Were you friends in high school?' inspire so much ducking and covering?" I asked Charlie the next morning over coffee at the diner.

"I know," he said. He looked fresher today, eyes brighter, his hair still wet from the shower. "When I asked my mom, I somehow ended up with a long list of the guys she'd dated or who had wanted to date her."

I laughed. "What did she say about my mom?"

"Nothing," he said. "She said 'Of course! She was a sweet girl! We were all friends, the whole gang of us. You know how small that school is.'"

"Did you tell her about the letter?"

"No. I was going to bring it up, but based on how well it went just asking her about someone who's still alive, it didn't seem like I was going to get anything asking about someone who was murdered."

"What about your dad?"

"No way. You know him. He's like the Stone Cove Island cruise director. He's already trying to spin how the hurricane is going to be great for the island's local businesses. You can't get a straight answer out of him. He only wants to talk about good news."

"Right," I said. "So no one wants to talk about Bess, and no one wants to talk about anyone who was friends with Bess and no one wants us to talk about Bess to anyone else. I just think that's bonkers."

"Maybe our moms are embarrassed that they're not

friends anymore. Who said don't talk about Bess to anyone?" he asked.

"My dad."

"No one told me not to."

I smiled. "Tricky. What were the Hardy Boys' names again? I'm kind of getting a Hardy Boys vibe from you right now. "

"Did they even have their own names? I was more of a Nate the Great kid."

"Right. I read those books. We call my dad that sometimes." I took a sip of coffee. It was good. The diner made arguably the best coffee on the island, even if the food was only okay. Outside the window, crews with scissor-lift trucks were cutting huge, half-downed trees into little pieces. There was going to be no shortage of firewood this winter, at least.

I looked across at Charlie, who was watching me, waiting for me to say more, but not in a way that was uncomfortable. It was odd, really, that it wasn't uncomfortable. It felt like we'd been doing this forever. He was funny, I thought. Much funnier than I'd ever realized when we were in school together. Weirdly, he made me feel funny too. I'd never thought of myself as funny.

"Maybe," I agreed. "I wish there was someone else we could show the letter to. Someone who would actually talk to us."

"There is," said Charlie. "Jay."

IT WAS A GOOD idea. I had given the original letter to my dad that morning over pancakes—Dad had rigged a propane hookup to our gas stove, so my mom was happily back on hot breakfast duty—but I had my calculus-book copy with me. I jumped up, ready to follow Charlie, then realized he was still sitting.

"We should pay first, don't you think?"

"Oh," I said, feeling like an idiot. "Right. Yeah." He signaled to Kelly, the waitress, who'd worked the off-season for as long as I could remember. I sat back down.

"Do you think I'll get in trouble with Officer Bailey for not taking the letter to her when I found it? That was why my dad thought we should turn it in."

"Do I think you'll get in trouble with Officer Bailey?" Charlie laughed. "Didn't she used to babysit for you?" She had, when I was in first or second grade. She hadn't been much fun as I remembered, but she was single, available and you couldn't really be any safer than with your own police bodyguard, right?

We walked over to the *Gazette* office. When we got there, Jay and Sparkler were working on closing a story for that afternoon's edition. Lawrence, Jay's proofreader, was there too, going over final copy. Jay welcomed us with a nod but stayed focused on his task. Sparkler trotted over, his nails click-clicking against the floor and kind of leaned against my knees. He was heavy and fleshy, where Salty was wiry and dense. I reached down and scratched in front of his ears. For some reason, I didn't want to show Jay the letter in front of Lawrence. Charlie seemed to have the same instinct, because he vamped on and on about the weather radar, FEMA gossip, ferry news and complaints about insurance companies he'd been hearing around town until Lawrence was gone.

"So kids," Jay said, rolling his chair closer to where we were standing, without getting up. "What can I do for you? Social visit? Or do you have a hot news tip for me?"

"Sort of neither," I began. "We wanted to ask you about something."

"Shoot," said Jay. "Not literally, of course." Charlie rolled his eyes. He'd had a lot more exposure to Jay's goofy sense of humor than I had and therefore had a lower tolerance.

"It's about the Bess Linsky murder," said Charlie. "You remember it? You were here then, right?"

"Do I remember it? Yeah. Biggest story/non-story the island ever had. I was deputy editor then. We had an actual staff in those days, before the Internet took over."

"Why do you say non-story?" I asked.

Jay looked exhausted. His eyes were bloodshot. "Well, maybe it was just timing. The murder—drowning. Whatever position you want to take on it. It happened in high season, August. It got to be really big news, really fast. The . . . consensus, I guess you'd have to call it . . . of people here—year-rounders, I mean—was that if the story didn't quiet all the way down during the off-season, the island was likely to have no future seasons. Ever."

"What?" said Charlie. "Didn't people want to know what happened? What about Bess's mother? She must have wanted to know."

"The mother moved to Gloucester right after it happened. I think that was the last straw for her, after Bess's dad, Grant, drowned. She was done with the island. There were no other relatives, just Grant's brother, Paul—from the marina, you know? But he's an unreliable witness or plaintiff or just about anything, right?"

I'd heard of Grant Guthy. He had owned the boat rental shop at the marina when my parents were kids. There were still pictures of him on the walls of the boatyard, holding a big fish, a big grin through his blond handlebar mustache. He was always photographed laughing or winking, usually in a loud print shirt. I could think of one where he wore a puka shell necklace, toasting the camera with a beer. From the little I'd heard of him, he was a partier, never married, good-looking and a flirt. I always thought he looked more like he belonged in a marina in San Diego or Hawaii than in a rocky cove in New England.

"People weren't clear on whether it was an accident or an actual murder," Jay went on. "They were never going to find her body. People sort of decided, better to save the future than solve the past."

"They found her hair chopped off and her clothes covered in blood and they thought it might be an accident?" I said in disbelief.

Jay shrugged. "I never said that was what I thought."

"And her dad drowned too?"

"Boating accident. Much less surprising, if you knew the guy."

"So you looked into it at the time? Bess, I mean?" asked Charlie.

"Sure," said Jay. "I tried to. But I was met with, let's say, strong resistance. As in, suddenly it went from everybody was talking about it to no one was talking about it. But that's typical Stone Cove. I've kinda learned my lesson by now. And anyway, it's water way under the bridge. You do know that it happened more than twenty years ago, right? What made you dig it up now?"

"We'd never even heard about it," I said. "Until I found this." I handed him my notebook, opened to the page where I'd copied the letter. "It's not the original, obviously. I found it cleaning up the lighthouse."

Jay took the notebook and scanned it. "Oh," he said. "Wow. Okay. Where's the original?"

"I gave it to my dad. He said we had to give it to Officer Bailey."

For a moment, Jay stood quiet, thinking. "Interesting. What did she say about it?"

"Nothing," I answered. "I mean, she hasn't talked to me about it yet."

"No? Huh. Okay. Listen, I'm going to give you two some advice that would get me kicked out of the New England Press Club if anyone heard it, but here it is: people did not want to talk about it then. That was made clear to me at the time. Twenty-five years later, and on the heels of a major hurricane, people are really not going to want to talk about it. I just want to prepare you for the reaction you're likely to get if you go showing this around the island. I'm not trying to tell you that you should or shouldn't."

Charlie and I waited for him to go on. He didn't.

"Don't you want to know what really happened?" Charlie said at last.

"Off the record? Of course I do." He went to a tall filing cabinet and riffled through the back of a drawer. Then he dropped a file folder, filled with scraps of paper and faded from green to a pucey, rotten lemon color.

"Here. My notes from the time. It's in bits and pieces, but you're welcome to look through them. They don't leave the building and I'm not officially helping. I really don't think there's anything to be done at this point anyway, or I would help."

"What if it was someone on the island?" It was a chilling thought, and I wasn't sure why I said it. Why should it be someone from the island? It could have been anyone, some random summer tourist Bess met in town. Or someone who came over on the ferry, looking for young girls to lure to the lighthouse.

Jay laughed. But it sounded off, like someone faking a cough. He looked away from us and started sorting papers on his desk. "It wasn't anyone from the island," he said. "Trust me."

SIX

If school on Tuesday felt weird for me, I could hardly imagine how weird it felt for Colleen and Abby and the other families sheltered here and wandering down the hall to first period. We weren't actually allowed into the gym— provisions were being made to hold team practices in the school yard, on the town green or at the Anchor Club, depending upon the sport—but it was awfully hard not to wonder what was going on in there. I was thankful, for the hundredth time, that our house was still standing. I was prepared to use the back door and live with mold forever, as long as I didn't have to camp out at school.

All morning, the teachers made a point of not talking about the hurricane and pretending things were normal. At eleven, I had a free period and I ducked into the library by myself. Meredith was occupied with AP Spanish. The school library kept a complete set of yearbooks too, and I easily found Bess's and pulled it off the shelf.

I stared at her picture. Her face was so open and yet unreadable. Was she hiding some illicit romance? A drug problem? A jealous rivalry? Some secret dark side? All appearances said no. Was she merely unlucky? In the wrong place at the wrong time? I scanned her activities. Theater and swim team. She was a good swimmer. Did that mean she was unlikely to drown or more likely to go for a swim by herself under dangerous conditions? I reminded myself about the hair and the blood. There was no way her death could have been a drowning accident. I only looked up when Lexy Morgan, Abby Whittle and Colleen walked in. Abby was wearing pajama pants. Like many of the kids camping out in the gym, she'd shown up to class like that. The teachers glared but seemed to feel too guilty to say anything under the circumstances, so they let it go. The girls saw me and wandered over to sit at my table. I closed the yearbook.

"Hey," I said as they joined me.

"Hey," they said back.

"Abby, is it like a giant sleepover in there?" I asked.

Abby grimaced. "Yeah. We're cooking FEMA s'mores every night. You should come hang out."

"I'm really sorry," I said. "This sucks."

"Yeah. It does. But on the plus side, I can get up half an hour later for school."

"Well, there's that," said Lexy. Her family had lost the candy store, but not their house. "Whatcha doing, Eliza?" I looked down at the yearbook sitting in front of me. Suddenly I felt self-conscious that about my obsession with this long-dead girl, in light of the immediate troubles now facing all of us. I improvised.

"Oh. It's an island history project I'm thinking about.

Did you guys ever hear about this girl who was murdered
in the late eighties?"

"No," said Lexy.

"Island legend," said Abby. "It's like the black anchor
myth. People talk about it but it never happened."

"This happened," I said, opening the yearbook. "Her
name was Bess Linsky. You never heard about this either?"

"There is no way there could be a murder here and we
wouldn't all know about it. This island is tiny."

"Seriously," I told her. "There were tons of news stories.
You can look it up."

Lexy looked pained. "God. One more thing I can't
Google. Is your Internet back up?"

"No," I said. "But the library's might be by now." I didn't
think I should mention Jay. The paper was, in actuality, the
only place where the Internet connection was working.
"What's the black anchor myth?"

"Oh," said Abby. "It's this thing they say about the old
days, when the island was much more uptight. There used
to be a book, like a registry of people who lived here. They
say if you did something upsetting—something people
didn't approve of, like wearing white after Labor Day or
maybe making bathtub gin; I don't really know what quali-
fied—someone would secretly deliver a black anchor to
your house and that meant get off the island. You're no
longer welcome. And they'd scratch your name out of the
registry." Abby was from a very old Stone Cove family. They
weren't well off, like the Penders, but they went way back.

"Shut up. There's no registry book," said Lexy.

"I know. I said it was a myth."

"That's creepy," said Colleen. Her family was newer to the island. Her parents had grown up in Gloucester and then moved here once they were married. "Even if it's not true."

Colleen had picked up the yearbook and was flipping through it. "Hey, awesome hair!" she said pointing at Cat Pender's picture. "Don't ever tell her I said that. Let's see whose dad was cutest in high school." She continued to page through. "Uh-oh. Eliza, I think that prize goes to you." There was my dad, looking so young and so hopeful. Looking at the picture made my eyes start to prickle and tear. What was wrong with me? There was something about his expression, something that was lost now. Or maybe gained. He looked not necessarily innocent but not . . . careful. That was it. Like Bess, his face was completely open, ready to face the future.

"Holy cow," said Lexy. "She's right. Your dad was a fox."

This was making me so uncomfortable. "Right. Ick. I have to get to fourth period. Meredith's probably waiting."

"Say hi to Charlie," said Colleen.

"What?" I said, thrown by the non sequitur.

"I saw you guys at the diner the other day," she said. "I guess maybe he is a joiner after all." I tried to return a cool, "ha-ha, very funny" smile, but the heat I felt all the way to my ears probably undermined the effect.

"See you guys," I managed, and bumbled out of the library.

Meredith hadn't heard about the murder either. It was starting to seem impossible that the island could keep such a public secret. I could understand why at the time, the scariness of the event combined with the potential scariness for the island's reputation had made people shy from the topic, but it had been twenty-five years, one generation agreeing not to talk resulting in the whole thing being excised from the island's history. I literally could not find one kid in school who knew anything about Bess.

I had English lit last period. Mr. Malloy pulled me aside as I was leaving and asked me to stay for a minute. I nodded to Meredith to go ahead without me. English was one of my best subjects, so I wasn't worried that I was in trouble exactly, but I did wonder what he could want. He sat down backward in the desk in front of mine to face me.

"Eliza. The school is in some turmoil, as you know, what with getting back to work after the storm, and the added complications of our housing situation here." I wondered if he'd heard about cleanup day, and was going to ask me to help organize something here at school.

"There is a lot of tension, a lot of rumors circulating, as I'm sure you've seen for yourself." I nodded. Now I did wonder if I was in trouble.

"So," he continued. "Today I heard buzzing around school concerning a rumor related to old island history. When I asked the student, she told me you had brought her the story. I want to suggest that this is perhaps not the time to stir up old pains, given the new pains we are all experiencing."

"Okay," I said. I looked directly at Mr. Malloy to try to figure out why this would upset or anger him, but his eyes were soft. "It's not a rumor though. I read about Bess's murder. It was all over the press."

"Stories like that can start to feel like ghost stories after a time," he said. "Even if they started as something real. I'm only telling you this to help you. When people are under a lot of stress, they can overreact to things they don't want to hear. Does that make sense?"

"Yes." It did. "Can I ask you something though?"

"Of course?" He said it like a question.

"Did you know Bess Linsky?" He was not one of the oldest teachers, but old enough to have been here in 1989 if he'd come to Stone Cove High early in his teaching career.

"I did. She was in my class one of my first years teaching here. She was an exceptionally bright girl."

"Did you—what do you think happened to her?"

He was silent. I felt awkward suddenly, like I'd asked too personal a question. He seemed to be thinking the same thing.

"I think," he began. "I think there is no way we can ever know."

AFTER SCHOOL, I DIDN'T know what to do with myself. Sailing practice had not started up again. The marina slips were still trashed and the boats weren't back in the water yet. If they didn't get them in soon it would be too late before it was too cold. Instead of heading downhill to my own house, I walked up, along Hill Road, which ran along the golf course past the Anchor Club. The club was housed in a beautiful building, huge and shingled and over a hundred years old. Famous architects who'd built grand houses in places like Newport, the Hamptons, and Fishers Island had designed it. Honestly, it was by far the grandest building we had, and not quite in character with the cottagey feel of the rest of Stone Cove.

In the center of the lawn was a giant anchor. It was black, but that was because it was made out of iron, I told myself, pretty standard for any big anchor. If there really had been a mysterious "Black Anchor Society," it had nothing to do with the Anchor Club, which was just a country club for golf, tennis and croquet—not that you could call that a sport. I wished, not for the first time, that my grandmother was still alive. She—my mother's mother—had been a potter and a great storyteller and a completely independent spirit. I could have asked her about the black anchors or about Bess without any shushing or sidestepping. She would have told me anything I wanted to know.

I thought about Mr. Malloy. I had spent just one day asking a few people at school about Bess's murder, and it had gotten right back to my teacher who had instantly warned me away. Was it because of the hurricane and everyone's nerves being on edge, or was there something about this story that set people off?

Continuing past the club, I suddenly found myself at the side entrance to the inn. I hadn't planned to see Charlie, but now, here I was. I wanted to get his reaction to Malloy and the kids at school. Maybe he would have a more objective take. I climbed the kitchen steps. Colleen and Charlie were sitting at the big farm table, snacking on banana bread. Colleen grinned her usual knowing grin at me and then made excuses about how busy she was. I joined Charlie at the table.

"How lucky are you that you aren't in school anymore?" I complained.

"Luck has nothing to do with it. It's talent," he said. "That combined with old age. Anyway, come January, I will be in school. Remember?" Right. He was starting at Northwestern.

"Yeah. That's different though. College." I said. "Hey, that doesn't leave you much more time at the *Globe*."

"Yeah," he said. He looked wistful, but I wasn't sure why. As far as I'd heard, Northwestern's journalism school had been his big dream forever. Maybe being at a real, live newspaper had made him anxious to get out into the world and get on with things. He cut a big piece of banana bread and handed it to me on a paper towel. "Here. Colleen makes this for the inn. My mom's recipe."

I took the banana bread. I was starving, I realized. "It's so good," I said, trying to hide my full mouth with my hand. "Wow."

"One of my mom's many secrets," he said. "Definitely one of my favorite secrets."

"Listen," I said. "I'm not interrupting, am I?"

Charlie smiled. "No way. How is life back at school? It must be super weird with kids living in the building."

I nodded. "Some showed up for class in pj's and slippers." He laughed. I went on. "I asked around a little about Bess. Just a few kids. And I didn't say anything about the letter."

"Yeah? Speaking of the letter, have you heard from Officer Bailey?"

"No," I said. "I'm sure she's busy with the storm cleanup.

But I think it's weird. I sort of want to get it over with, whatever she's going to say to me."

"It'll be fine." For a second he put his hand over mine on the table. It was warm and dry. I hoped mine didn't feel greasy or sticky from the banana bread. Then he moved it away. "Eliza, you didn't do anything wrong."

"I know," I said. "But somehow, every time the subject comes up, I feel like I'm trespassing or something. Like today, I brought up the murder with a couple of girls I saw in the library, Meredith, some sailing team kids and then with my chemistry lab partner. I just wanted to know if they'd ever heard about it. By the end of the day, Mr. Malloy—did you have him for English? You must have, right?" Charlie nodded.

"So, Mr. Malloy pulls me aside after class this afternoon and tells me not to start rumors and get people all upset."

"That's kind of weird," Charlie said. "I think of him as one of the more easygoing teachers. What'd you find out talking to people?"

"Nothing. No one had ever heard anything about it." I watched to see if he would react the same way I had.

"You're kidding," he said after it had all sunk in. He knew I wasn't. "Wow. I don't even know how you—how is that possible? Everyone on the island agreed not to talk about it and it's never come up again? In twenty-five years?"

"I know," I said. "That's why I feel so—I'm kind of freaking out." There weren't many boys I could confess something like that to, but at that moment with Charlie, I didn't hesitate.

"Don't worry," he said. "It was a long time ago. Nothing

like that has happened since. I think everyone feels stirred up by the storm, right? That's why Malloy was weird with you. That's why it's getting to us more than it would normally."

"You too?" I asked. He nodded. I sort of wished he would take my hand again. "Don't let that get around though. I don't want to wreck my rep. And I hear you like to spread rumors." Now I wanted to smack him, not hold hands. I laughed.

"What rep, Charlie? Your loner, misanthrope intellectual poet rep?"

"I had one poem published—ONE—in the *Stone Cove Quarterly* in eleventh grade." It was a joke, our school's literary journal. There were so few of us, they basically made everyone write something to submit. But you didn't have to write a poem. And they weren't all chosen.

"Right," I said. "I remember that poem. I'm sure it was way beyond me, because I was a dopey little tenth grader. But it actually did seem pretty good."

Charlie hesitated, his lips parted, like he was working up a snappy comeback. Then instead of speaking, he reached across the table and kissed me. I was so startled, I froze. You know how they say when you're about to die your life flashes in front of you? A similar jumble of confused images played a montage in front of my eyes. The experience was much more pleasant than dying, obviously. It felt like it went on a long time, but it was probably a second. I didn't breathe. I saw moments of the past week, moments of Charlie as a child, all the time we'd spent together then with no significance, so much a premonition of now. I felt my own confusion. Was I here right now by accident or my own unconscious plan? All this wondering about Bess, the research in the library, coffee in the diner— was it all just an excuse to kiss Charlie? And if I did kiss Charlie, if that's what I'd wanted but had not known that I wanted, what would that mean now? Would we stay friends if things didn't work out? Would it make the short time he had left on the island fraught with pressure and dread? Would I spend the rest of my senior year pining in my room and wishing I'd never run into him? I did not know the answer to any of these questions.

"Eliza. You all right?" He was looking at me with concern, I saw, waiting for me to say something. Before I could think of how to respond, I leaned across the table and kissed him back. And then his mother walked in.

I don't know if Cat Pender was standing in the door watching us for a long time or if she came in that second. All I knew was, one minute I was lost in warm, soft, wool-and-sandalwood soap-scented Charlieland, the next my eyes were wide open and we were both sitting as far away from each other as possible, staring at his mother in horror.

"Oh, Eliza," Cat fumbled. "I didn't see you there. Anyway, Charlie, I do need your help this afternoon, as we planned." She looked at me as she said this, not Charlie. I believe "pointedly" is the expression? It was clear I was expected to go. Charlie and I exchanged twin, embarrassed grins and I backed my way out of the kitchen, making excuses about homework and complimenting the banana bread. That earned me a tight smile, as Cat waited for me to leave.

I didn't walk home so much as bounce. I felt jitters, both inside and outside of my body. Why had I kissed him? Is that what I'd had in mind when I'd gone to the inn? What was Charlie thinking now? What was I thinking now? I needed Charlie, I thought, as an ally. He was the only person I could talk to about this crazy Bess business. He was the only person who understood my growing obsession with it and the questions it raised about my mother, his mother, both of our parents in fact. But I was also attracted to him. Clearly.

If we became involved, and things went badly, I would have no one to confide in. I would have Meredith, but she wasn't involved in the same way. If we got together, it would have to end badly, I realized. He would go back to Boston soon. He would leave for Northwestern soon after that and probably never come back. *Slow down,* I told myself. It was just a kiss. An impulse. Two people acting crazy during a crazy time. This sort of thing happened. I remember my dad telling stories about seeing strangers hooking up in the aftermath of September 11th, about how the air was charged with what he called "apocalyptic energy." Besides, a kiss was not a marriage proposal.

My skin felt hot, but my fingers and toes felt cold. Was I going to faint? No. Absolutely not.

I stopped and sat down on a rock. I needed some perspective. I was getting way ahead of myself. I needed to just calm down and wait and see how things played out— exactly the thing I was worst at.

SEVEN

I sat in my room alone and forced myself to focus on homework instead of the crazy afternoon. My phone sat on my
desk next to my chemistry notebook, punishing me with
its silence. My parents had gone out. Dad volunteered as
a coach of the high school swim team, and he had a team
dinner. Mom had gone with him. She never went to things
like that. I chose to take it as a good sign.

The electricity had gone out again. Dad had rigged
battery-powered work lanterns around the house before
he'd gone, but it meant I couldn't use my computer and my
cell phone's battery would be dead soon. It also meant no
hot water. It was almost more demoralizing for the power
to go out again now that it had been restored, but I was
getting the idea that this was how it was going to be for a
while, everything on and off. That was certainly how it was
with food in the grocery store these days. The transport
schedule was cut severely by the loss of the ferry, and the big
ships couldn't come all the way into the harbor, so the fresh
fruits and vegetables looked sad and less than plentiful.

As long as we still had a supply of propane, our stove was our most reliable appliance, so Mom had been compulsively baking: applesauce bread, pumpkin bread, zucchini bread (sad zucchini worked fine for this). Normally at this time of year she obsessively made soup, so I was glad she'd found another outlet during our current situation. Things are always much better when she's kept busy. Maybe I could get her Cat Pender's banana bread recipe.

Instead of algebra II or chemistry, I was thinking about Charlie. Or, more precisely, I was wondering what Charlie was thinking of me. How premeditated had that kiss been for either of us? Had I missed some undercurrent all these hours we'd been hanging out? Now that it had happened, I couldn't stop dwelling on it, of course. It felt weird that I had left so abruptly before we could a) do it some more, or b) at least talk about it. He hadn't texted me. I checked my phone for the hundredth time. Seventeen percent battery left until who knew when the electricity would be restored. Did I have to wait to hear from him? I didn't, right? I tapped a quick text onto the screen and hit SEND before I could reconsider. hiya. sorry i had to run. so weird with your mom! you ok? I reread it. The exclamation point looked dorky. Too late.

I set the phone back down and watched it. Nothing happened. I went to the kitchen and took a couple of graham crackers from a glass jar. They were a little stale, but I didn't really mind. Then I went back to my room to recheck the still-blank screen on my text messages. *Come on, Charlie!* What was he doing? I flopped onto my bed with my phone in hand. Salty jumped up and curled up behind my knees. Thirteen percent. I closed my eyes just as the phone buzzed. A text from Charlie. yeah. sorry about that. Sorry about what? I shook the phone. I stared at it, waiting for more. Sorry about his mom walking in? Sorry about kissing me? I wrote, maybe jay or library aft. school tom.? He wrote back, don't think i can. told dad would help here. sorry.

Sorry, sorry, sorry. What was he so sorry about suddenly? Hadn't he kissed me first? I waited for another text that never came. I changed for bed. I took a halfhearted stab at my problem set. Then I heard my parents come in. My mom was speaking to my dad in a quiet, urgent whisper. I couldn't make out anything she said. He shushed her and the house fell silent a moment before he called out to me.

"Eliza? It's almost eleven."

"Okay, Dad." I climbed into bed and clicked off the lantern. My cell phone had run down completely. I was tired of circling around inside my head. Maybe I would figure it all out tomorrow.

In the morning, the house was deserted. Dad hadn't made coffee, which was unusual, but maybe he had to be on the job site extra early. He was working on replacing the roof at the Anchor Club. The job was proving to be a pain, he'd told me, because of all the landmark preservation rules that went along with that building. Jimmy Pender was head of the historic preservation committee for the island and he treated it like a religion. I felt a little hurt that Dad hadn't waited for me. I tended to get up early and we usually had coffee together in the morning (Mom, a late riser and a tea drinker, did not join us). But okay, I would get dressed, twist up my hair into something that could pass as a hairstyle instead of a dirty-hair cover-up—which was the reality—and get coffee at the Picnic Basket before school. If I couldn't find out more about Bess at school, my best bet was to seek out the island's biggest talkers.

I biked to town, since that detour would add extra time to my trip to school. The air was misty and humid and thick with ocean. I could feel it forming a cool, salty film on my skin. In the harbor, there were huge, orange dredging machines of a kind I had never seen before. Almost every store along Water Street was still closed, but most were now boarded up and safe from the weather. That was good, I thought. At the moment we were having weird, semitropical weather, but in my experience, that could turn quickly to dry, bitter cold. I parked my bike outside the Picnic Basket. In the off-season especially, there was no reason to lock anything up.

It was early. Nancy was still arranging pastries on the counter, and Greg was filling the coffee urns. No one else was in the shop yet. I was glad to have caught them alone.

"Hi, dear," said Greg. "Coffee'll be finished in two minutes."

"You guys must be so busy these days," I said, picking up a raisin twist in a piece of wax paper and showing Nancy, so she could ring it up. "You're, like, the only game in town."

"Just about," said Nancy. "I wake up every day and thank the stars we made it through. It just hurts to see how everybody's suffering, doesn't it?" I nodded.

"I know," I said. "This must be the worst thing that's

ever happened to Stone Cove." Okay, so I was baiting her. I thought I saw Greg give Nancy a look, but not quickly enough to stop her reply.

"It's right up there with Bess Linsky, that's for sure."

"The girl who drowned, right?" I prompted.

"Was killed. Yes. It was just terrible. That poor girl."

"Did you know her?"

"We all knew her. But she and her mom kept to themselves. Karen did most of her shopping at the marina mart. Didn't come into town that much. And Bess was a nice girl, but not, you know, a real island girl like you or Meredith." I must have looked blank, because she continued. "She wasn't a joiner. Wasn't so much part of things, like your family is, or some of the other old families." Wasn't a joiner? I couldn't help thinking of Charlie. Everyone kept saying he wasn't a joiner, but that didn't seem to be a problem for him. And my parents? My mom was closer to a shut-in than a joiner. I let Nancy go on.

"Maybe if she'd taken Grant's name it would have made some difference. But probably not. I thought Karen should take her back to Gloucester after Grant's accident. This isn't an easy place for a single mom, you know." I couldn't think of any single moms on Stone Cove Island. I could see how you might stand out in that situation.

"What happened to Grant?" I asked, though I already knew the answer.

"He drowned too," said Nancy. "But that was hardly a surprise. The way he and his buddies drank and went out on those boats."

"He was out with friends when it happened?" I asked.

Nancy seemed doubtful for a moment. She looked at Greg to confirm.

"Not that day, I don't think. Wasn't he alone, Greg?"

"Think so," agreed Greg. The coffee was done and Greg poured me a large cup. I accepted it gratefully.

"It's always interesting to hear the old stories," I said, hoping that I was coming off as curious, not pushy. "About the island's history."

"Your dad knows just as much," said Nancy with a modest blush. She liked to be thought of as the island historian, I could tell.

"Poor Bess," I said, redirecting the conversation. "She was alone too? Swimming, I mean?"

"Well, she was alone before she ended up in the lighthouse. No one knows much after that. They did find her clothes. And her hair." Nancy made a face at that.

"Who found them?" I asked.

She looked blank, as though she'd never considered that part of the story. "I don't know," she said, sounding surprised at herself. "Do you remember, Greg?"

"Kids, I think. Kids who went surfing the next day. Don't remember exactly who." Huh. That seemed like something I could look into. The door jangled as Mr. Morgan came in with Jimmy Pender.

"I'd better go," I said. "Or I'll be late for school."

"Nice chatting with you, Eliza. Morning, Jimmy. Morning, Ned."

As I had not been able to charge my cell phone, I could not check to see if I'd gotten any late night or early morning texts from Charlie. As far as I knew, he was busy today, and I didn't know when I would see him again. Running into Jimmy Pender had made me feel self-conscious, as though I were stalking their family, though of course I had gotten to the Picnic Basket first. Jimmy was as friendly as usual, but I resisted asking anything about Charlie and what they were busy with that day.

ALL DAY AT SCHOOL, I kept my head down. I stayed away from old yearbooks, I asked no probing questions. In English class though, I still felt Mr. Malloy's eye on me. As class was ending, he stopped at my desk and put a hand down, fingers spread.

"She was wonderful in *The Crucible*. Played Goody Proctor. She really seemed to inhabit the role, as they are fond of saying in theater reviews. And she was a very good writer. That is what I remember most," he said. His voice was low. I looked up, surprised.

"You asked about Bess." His eyes were reddish and watery, like he'd been in a smoke-filled room. His shoulders drooped a little, as he leaned his weight onto my desk. "She was a very good writer. That's the thing that stands out in my memory. One paper in particular I remember. I've sometimes used it as an example in my European literature class."

He straightened up and seemed to wake up from whatever reverie had taken him over. Then he nodded at me curtly, to say I was dismissed, and walked back to his desk at the front of the classroom.

I HAD PLANNED TO go to the town library on my way home to look at news stories again. I wanted to find out who had discovered Bess's bloody clothes and hair. Instead I went home. I wasn't sure why staying away from Charlie felt connected to staying away from the Bess story, but somehow it did. It was like being on some kind of diet. I had to abstain from it all.

But as soon as I got home, I realized it was a mistake. I was bored. The power was still out. I didn't want to do my homework. I was still thinking about Charlie and I was still thinking about Bess's murder.

I reread Bess's letter. The phrases: *do not await the last judgment; it takes place every day*; and *to breathe is to judge* still stood out to me as odd, like it had been written by a different person from the rest of the letter. Was it possible more than one person had committed her murder? Could it have been two people? A group of people?

I wandered from room to room, looking for a distraction. Salty trotted after me. I picked up a new book my dad was reading about a sailing rescue at sea. Normally I liked those kinds of stories, but I closed this after reading a page or two.

I moved to Mom's closet. Nowadays she dressed in the neutral-colored, tastefully generic, linen and knit clothes a much older woman might wear, but she had kept her dresses and bags from when she was younger. I liked to take them out and look at them. We had the same size feet, and I would try on her old shoes. Now I put on some white patent-leather sandals, with wide straps that crossed in front and buckled at the ankle. I'd never seen Mom actually wear any heels this high. I could barely walk in them.

The top of the closet was where she kept her old purses.

There was an alligator satchel—not real, I was sure—shaped like a doctor's bag, a leather saddlebag in black and light brown leather. Another bag seemed to be made of an old kilim rug. I was looking for one in particular, an evening bag. It was black and rectangular, with a flap held shut by a gold panther, curled in a *C* shape. I loved this purse, partly because it fascinated me to imagine why she'd bought it and where she'd taken it. It was the kind of bag ladies in New York took with them to dinner in fancy uptown bistros. My mother had rarely been as far as Boston. I would take it down and look at it periodically, trying to imagine the person my mother had been when she'd worn it across her thin shoulder.

This time I had trouble finding it. It wasn't on the shelf in its soft protective cover, where it usually was. I finally located it in a shoe box at the bottom of a stack. As I slid the box out, I accidentally pulled the boxes resting on top and the whole pile rained down on my head. Salty leaped away and hid under my parents' bed. I swore as I hopped off the step stool I'd dragged from the kitchen and tried to put the closet back the way I'd found it. The panther bag had skidded out of its open box and was resting, open and clasp down, on the floor. Damn. I hoped I hadn't scratched the leather. I righted it carefully and went to click it shut. As I did, I saw that the bag wasn't empty. Inside was a small, plain black sketchbook, the kind art students carry around. I opened it to the first page. The date, April 10, 1989, was printed across the top of the page in my mom's very girly, very recognizable handwriting. I knew instantly it was her diary.

EIGHT

Almost any diary is irresistible, but the diary of my own mother, this person who was so shut off and incomprehensible to me, a window into her thoughts and even better, her thoughts at my age? I didn't even hesitate. Before I dove in, I did make sure the closet was put back exactly as I had found it. Then I went out the newly functional back door and sat on the old wood swing my dad had made when I was a kid. If I read the diary in my room, I might be surprised by my parents' return and be cornered, but out here, I could see the driveway and escape through the backyard if I needed to. I could hide the diary in the shed. No, not in the shed. My dad's workshop was in the shed. But someplace. At any rate, this would give me more options.

"April of 1989," I murmured, working backward in my head. My mother would have been seventeen. Her birthday was in the fall, late September. I thought back to her most recent birthday celebration, which had taken place just a few weeks earlier, right before the storm. Flowers from my dad. Maybe a sweater? I couldn't even remember what his gift to her had been. I had given her a bottle of perfume, same one she always wore, same as every year. Dinner at home, as usual. It blurred with every other past birthday. That April, the April of the diary, she would have been exactly as old as I was now. I opened the book to the first page and began to read.

Perfect day today. A on history test. Warm enough for no coat. Yay! Finally spring. Such a long winter.

So, even at seventeen my mother was boring. I trudged onward, prepared for further tedium, and found it.

Jimmy asked Cat to the Anchor Club Spring Fling. She said no. I really don't get it, since all she's talked about all winter is going to the stupid dance with him. She says I don't understand how the game is played. Her theory is now he'll really want to go with her. What I think is he'll ask someone else. But she's the expert.

Cat. The first page of her diary, and it really does sounds like Cat is her best friend. It was impossible to picture it.

What do I know? Or care. It's just a party. Two apples. One yogurt. 3/4c popcorn. Piece of chicken for dinner (half). Weight: 108. 372 steps to the end of our block. Teeth = 74 brushstrokes.

Whoa. The diary swerved suddenly off the rails into new, dark territory. This was my mother? This was what was inside her seventeen-year-old brain? Her current brain?

Talked to 11 people today, incl. 2 strangers.

I tried not to let it throw me, but it did. My mother did not just sound nervous, stressed-out or tightly wound. She did not seem just a little shy. She sounded crazy. I had thought I wanted a glimpse inside Mom's world. Now that I'd entered, I felt stifled, hot and uncomfortable. I decided to skip ahead to see if her entries from August would reveal any facts, beyond how many calories she'd taken in and how many cracks in the sidewalk she'd stepped over.

There were several entries for August, most of them short and disjointed. They included abbreviations I couldn't decode:

LB invited us to sleepover. Bess said yes before I could stop her. Cat will have cow now and make things even worse. B hung out at beach all day with N. Wanted to know if I think he likes her? Doesn't everybody? Wish I could be B. Not care what people think. Say things like "school is a waste of time." He's nice. I think B likes him more than J. That would solve Cat's problems, right? And he's never going to notice me with B around.

Another one read: *Was supposed to go to Jimmy's party with Cat and Bess. Right before, it happened again. Had to stay home. Cat and Bess were mad at me. Can't explain to them what it feels like. Thought Bess would understand, but she doesn't. Oh well. They're better off without me. Everyone will be better off without me.*

Each entry ended with similar compulsive stats: *Weight 105. 1 cottage cheese plus 8 grapes, 3 Triscuits. Diet soda counts? 152 sit-ups. Walked to lighthouse and back. 82 stairs. Talked to 4 people, 1 stranger.* Or *Weight 107. Gum, 2 apples, popcorn, 3 bites ice cream, ½ hamburger. Ferry dock 387 boards = to entrance gate. Talked to 0 people.*

I was scared now, of my mom or for my mom, I wasn't sure which. But I couldn't put the book down, however much I wanted to. Why had she kept this horrible documentation of her past? Did she actually want to remember being this way? Was she *still* this way? It was an unbearable thought. Finally I reached the date of Bess's murder. There was a long entry, written about a week later. This one was different. It read more like . . . a eulogy? It was impossible to imagine the Willa of this diary standing in front of a crowd, delivering a eulogy. It was more like an apology. A confession.

It was my fault that she was murdered. The night Bess died, she left the bar at the marina late. She would have had a couple of drinks, not enough to get drunk. She would have danced, maybe with Jimmy, maybe with Nate, maybe with some older guy we didn't know. She would have walked home alone. Unless I was sleeping over, she always walked home alone. She was mad at me that night . . .

Bess had been too good a swimmer to drown. Not too good a swimmer to get caught in a riptide; too good a swimmer to go swimming alone on a moonless night in the Atlantic Ocean. Her clothes were found in the lighthouse, covered in blood. Her killer had cut off all her hair. Some people said a huge anchor had been painted across the front door of their house. Others said that was only a rumor. I never saw it. I didn't go to her house again after that night. Her body was never found.

Her mother refused to talk about Bess afterward. She got rid of all her stuff. I wanted to keep something to remember her, but Karen said no. I knew that Bess had been scared before she died. She had shown me—just me, she told me—the letter.

I only read it once. But I can still remember every word. "Uninvited guest," it began and then later, "down came a blackbird and pecked off her nose." The more I tried to push that line from my mind, the more fiercely it returned, and I couldn't not picture her face. I hoped he had not done anything to her face. I should have

gone with Bess to The Slip that night. I should have told someone
about the letter. But I never did.

I closed the diary.

Now I knew three things:

1. My mom was more of a stranger than I'd even imagined.
2. She had read the same letter twenty-five years ago. Not only had she read it, but Bess had read it before she was murdered.
3. Mom had wanted to know as badly as I did what had really happened to Bess.

I wondered if she still did.

I took the diary into my room and found a place to hide it behind the low bookcase. I was going to read more later, of course, but mostly I took it to protect my mom. I didn't like the idea of these terrible words and memories sleeping in the same room with her. Which was insane, obviously. They were *her* words and memories. But somehow they seemed too awful to live with.

I wanted to talk to Charlie. Of course I realized the proverbial ball was in his proverbial court, but still, he was the only person I could really talk to about this. He was the only other person who had this much information about Bess's murder, who would understand it. *This,* I told myself, *is exactly why you shouldn't have kissed him. You need him. You need to be able to talk to him. You need him to help you figure this out. You don't need to kiss him. You can kiss Josh, or whoever.* I wanted to kiss Charlie though. I knew that. And now it seemed like I had neither option. It was nine o'clock. My parents still weren't home. I couldn't think of anything else to do. I went to bed, nagged by the feeling that somehow I might turn out just like my mother.

NINE

True to her core belief in the hot breakfast, Mom was making eggs when I came into the kitchen the next morning. She put a plate down in front of me, without asking if I wanted any.

"Thanks," I said. "Mom, you're such a social butterfly these days." She flashed me a confused and then alarmed look. "I mean, you went out two nights in a row. When does that ever happen?"

"There was a town council meeting last night," she said, turning back to the counter. "Your dad wanted to go. You know I hate those things, but it's important, because of the hurricane. We need to know what's coming for the winter." I nodded. Charlie's parents were on the town council. Why did my every thought now circle me back to Charlie? I redirected my brain as Mom broke four more eggs into the bowl.

"Didn't Dad already go to work?"

She looked down at the eggs. There would be too many now. "Oh. Yes. I guess that's right." But she kept stirring them anyway. I wondered if she was counting each stir, if she needed to reach a certain number before she could stop. I rinsed my plate and picked up my book bag.

"Will you be home after school?" she asked.

"I don't know." I improvised. "I might go study at the library."

Mom nodded, still focused on the eggs. "Have a nice day," she said.

On the way out, I detoured back through my room and grabbed the diary from its hiding place behind the bookcase.

MEREDITH WAS ONLY FREE for the first half of lunch. She had a college admissions meeting. Since I was applying only to in-state schools that used the common application, I didn't have to go. The schools Meredith was applying to had more complicated requirements, different essays and interviews. It was a warm day, so we sat at the picnic benches in front of the school.

"Halloween's getting closer," she said. "Did you decide who you're going with?"

I looked at her. I had decided who I wanted to go with, but that didn't mean it was going to happen. What I would not do, I was sure, was follow Cat's hard-to-get strategy. I agreed with my mother, at least on that point. Thinking about this took me back to Mom's diary. Who had Jimmy taken to the dance in the end? Maybe Cat had won. They ended up married, after all. I'd have to go back and read more.

"I'm thinking of asking Tim McAllister," I said finally, poking her in the ribs.

"Ha. Ha," she shot back. "Hilarious. Cradle robber."

"I really am going to ask him for you, if you don't get it together soon."

"Don't," she said, looking suddenly serious. She pulled her knees up and rested her chin on them. It was a very Meredith gesture, one she'd done as a little girl too. It meant, *I give up*. "I probably can't go anyway."

"What? You have been talking about nothing else since school started. In fact, if you're not going to go, I want all that time we spent discussing it back. Plus interest."

"I still want to," she said. "But I might have to go do my college auditions early. My parents are worried that if they don't get the ferry running before the harbor freezes, it's going to be almost impossible to get back and forth to the mainland this winter. Normally I wouldn't have to go in until January or February. But I might go this month, if Barnard and Juilliard can reschedule me. I'm so bummed though. It's our last fall. I just wanted to do all the regular island things, one last time."

"I know," I said. Everyone's life was turned upside down right now, and some of my classmates who planned to go far away for college, like Meredith, would leave with this broken memory of the island, instead of the image of their home the way it was supposed to be.

"Damn," she said, flipping over her phone. "It's twelve thirty. I have to go to that meeting. Sure you don't want to come?"

"They said for UMass and local schools we don't have to."

"I know, but don't you want to anyway, in case you change your mind? And to be a good friend and keep me company?"

"No way," I answered.

She stuck her tongue out at me. "Rude."

"Okay," I amended. "No *thank you*. And you're the one sticking your tongue out at people."

"See you later," she laughed, dragging her heavy backpack behind her. Meredith always chose practical over fashionable. Her backpack looked like something you could take on an Antarctic expedition. It looked hilarious on her ballerina frame.

"Have fun," I said. Then she was gone and I was alone. I took out my mother's diary. I held a pencil as a prop, so I could act like I was sketching if someone came too close and got curious. I flipped back to May, around the date of the Spring Fling. Jimmy had ended up going with Bess after Cat turned him down. Naturally, Cat was furious with Bess, who was supposed to realize that Cat liked Jimmy and turn *him* down. I was familiar with that type of girl logic. Mom had gone with Dad "just as friends"—right, Mom. Cat had ended up going with someone named Brian. There were no last names and sometimes my mom referred to people by their initials, so it was hard to know who she was talking about. At the actual dance however, Cat had disappeared with Jimmy, leaving Bess in an awkward threesome with my parents. Some girl called Lynn started to tag along and offered to give Mom a ride home. Mom was annoyed but didn't want to hurt Lynn's feelings. Dad ended up taking Bess home. Mom was bummed (served you right for going as "friends," Mom. So chicken.) and felt even worse the next day when Cat made fun of her for getting stuck with

Loser Lynn instead of the guy she actually liked, and bragged about how she'd won Jimmy's devotion.

It was practically a soap opera. You could diagram the drama that Cat had caused: turning down the guy she liked, then breaking up his date to make him go off with her. I still didn't get why that was better than just agreeing to go with him in the first place, but perhaps Cat had access to feminine wiles I didn't. Or maybe the point was to show Bess she couldn't have Jimmy. Could that have played into it? That she'd wanted to get the guy she liked and put her friend in her place at the same time? The next day of course, my mom was in a gloom, walked on the beach alone, called Bess, etc.

I skipped Mom's OCD footnotes for this passage and moved on to July and August. It was clear Mom had some better weeks than others. Sometimes she sounded like any shy, insecure teenager. She went to Bess's house for sleepovers. Nate took both of them sailing. There were beach bonfires (I guess I'd been wrong about that one), long days sunbathing slathered in baby oil instead of sunscreen. Other weeks Mom holed up in her room, listening to The Cure and the Cowboy Junkies set to repeat on her new CD player. She starved, weighed, and counted a lot during these periods.

It was surprising to me how little she mentioned Dad or any of her own crushes. Her diary devoted way more time to Cat's manipulations of Jimmy, Cat's jealousy when Bess would talk to him at a party, and Cat's opinions of who at Stone Cove High was and wasn't worth their time. Cat, at seventeen, seemed to me to have been a classic mean girl, and I didn't see that she'd changed all that much since. I wondered if Mom got sick of it or if eventually Cat had turned against her. Something had broken up their friendship long before I was born.

SCHOOL WAS CREAKILY GETTING back to a modified normal. We had assemblies in the cafeteria and gym in the playground. Several times a day, the power flickered off and then whirred back on at half strength, fueled by loud generators. To me, the changes made little difference, but then I wasn't living in the gym and taking showers in the girls' locker room. I had already given Mom the excuse of going to the library after school, so I decided I would actually do that. In town, I noticed the village green had been cleared of fallen branches, but the grass was still burnt yellow. I wondered if it would grow back on its own or if they would have to re-sod the whole thing in the spring. It looked painful, if plants could experience pain.

At the library, the power was back on and the Internet was up. That meant I could skip the microfiche. It also meant way more people were using the library. I signed my name to the waiting list for a computer terminal, and went out to sit on the front steps and wait. *Into the Wild* was in my bag and I was only a few pages in when I looked up to see Charlie approaching the entrance. I had planned to be cool the next time I saw him, but I couldn't stop my grin.

"Hi," I said, standing quickly. "How are you?"

"Good." He stopped at the bottom of the steps and looked up at me, warily I thought.

"The Internet is working again. I was going to look up

some news articles about the investigation. Greg Jurovic told me Bess's things were discovered at the lighthouse by some surfers. If we can figure out who it was, maybe we can ask them about it." As soon as I said "we" I regretted it. Charlie had an expression on his face that indicated he was not in the mood to be a "joiner" after all. What had I done? I wondered. We both grew uncomfortable as a long silent moment lingered between us.

"Cool," he said. "I'm actually here to help Mary Ellen with the library's computer archiving setup. They want to make sure they have everything backed up properly, since the power keeps going out."

Cool? That didn't even sound like Charlie. Had he had a lobotomy since I'd last seen him?

"Very cool," I said tonelessly. "You'd better not keep Mary Ellen waiting then." I gave him a frosty stare and waited for him to go. It was the exact opposite of what I wanted. For an instant, I felt as crazy as my seventeen-year-old mother.

"Yeah," he said. His voice was so soft I could barely hear him. "I should go." He walked slowly up the steps, not turning back. I felt like an idiot. I waited for as long as I thought it would take him to get to the librarian's office, then added another eight minutes, so there was no danger of running into him again. I was never going to kiss another boy, that was for sure.

As I walked back into the main room, people looked up. I might have been stomping a little, I guess, or maybe they could feel the humiliation radiating off me. I sat down at terminal 3 and logged in with a few quick clicks.

One thing I couldn't understand was how Charlie, with his journalist's instincts, could have lost interest in Bess's story. Losing interest in me, fine. But I knew he'd been just as consumed as I was with wanting to know what really happened on the beach that night. I knew he itched to find out why our mothers no longer spoke.

The *Providence Journal* had covered the investigation the most closely of all the newspapers, at least as far as they could follow it. I found an account from a few days past the murder that reported three surfers had gone to the police after coming across the dead girls' things. One had been Bess's uncle, Paul Guthy. He was Grant's younger brother. The paper listed his age as twenty-eight and said he'd been surfing on East Beach at the time of the discovery. The two boys who had actually found Bess's clothes had ducked into the lighthouse, looking for a place to change into their wet suits. One was Billy Landron, a boy from a summer family who had owned a big house on the bluffs. I knew his daughters from sailing camp, but the family had sold the house when they moved to London a few years ago.

The other was Jimmy Pender.

I had to read that twice to be sure I wasn't imagining it. Charlie's dad. I couldn't believe he'd actually found Bess's bloody clothes, taken Bess to dances and Charlie had never heard a thing about her. I wondered if that was Cat's mandate, or Jimmy's, or something they decided together. I wanted to run back to the librarian's office, grab Charlie and show him the article. Of course I couldn't do that. I also couldn't talk to Jimmy, who was not going to tell me anything about this when he'd never even mentioned it to

his own children. His friend Billy Landron was long gone.
But I did know where to find Paul Guthy.

I SHOULD HAVE CHECKED in at home before heading all the way out
to the marina. I knew I would make my mom worried. But
I didn't. Instead I stopped by just long enough to grab
my bike without going inside. It had cooled off a lot since
the strange, humid, warm weather we'd had earlier in the
week, and it was suddenly getting dark a lot earlier. Winter
was coming. I tried not to think about what would happen
to all of us if it arrived before the island had gotten the
basic necessities back in place.

By the time I was on the road, I had warmed up from the
exertion of biking. Only my fingers were really cold. It was
quiet on the road. I saw only one car, heading the other way,
into town. The power was out on this side of the island,
and the streetlights were dark. I felt that strange vertigo
you sometimes get, watching my single bike headlamp
peer into the blank darkness. If you looked a certain way,
up started to feel like down and down like up. I kept imagining sounds coming from behind me: the crush of dry
leaves, rustling in the trees. When I looked, no one was
there. I shook it off. *Deer,* I thought, *or raccoons.* Just past
sunset was a busy time of day in the animal world, when
the night hunters came out to look for prey and the day
timers looked for a safe spot to sleep.

The marina was lit with the dim, brownish light I'd come
to recognize as generator produced. No one had bothered to put their boats back in the water after the storm
here, though the slips were much less damaged than in

the harbor. It was too close to the end of the season. I wondered what there was for Paul Guthy to do out here at this time of year. He worked as the caretaker of the marina. Grant had owned the business, but now the town ran it.

Paul was there tonight, I could see through the office window. He had his back to me, his feet up on a chair, while he watched football on TV and drank a beer. I leaned my bike against a dock piling and rapped gently on the door as I opened it. There was no one else here, and I didn't want to startle him.

Paul turned to glare at me but kept one eye on the game.

"Yeah?" he said. He said it like he wasn't particularly interested in what I might say.

"Hi," I started, realizing I had come with no plan. I didn't know Paul, except by sight. I was here to ask him about his niece's murder twenty-five years ago. For all I knew, he was a suspect at the time. For all I knew, he was the one who had killed her. Wasn't it true that most violent crimes took place between people who knew each other, and even more often, people who were related? There was no tactful way to start the conversation.

"Hi," I started over. I decided to go with a lie. "I'm doing a research paper for school about island history. I know your family has been on Stone Cove a long time, and your, uh, business has been really important to the island?" Why was I making it a question? Paul grunted. It could have meant "go on" or "get out." I really couldn't tell.

"Your family's owned the marina boatyard for a long time?"

He stood up now, staggering a little and I realized he was drunk. He lumbered toward me, just a step or two, and glared harder. "What do you want?" he said. His question didn't sound like a question.

"I'm a senior at Stone Cove High and—"

"I know who you are," he said. I didn't know if that was true. "You got some nerve, coming here to ask about my family, our business, when you know they took it and your family's part of them that did."

"Do you mean, now that the town runs it? My family's not part of the town council."

"It was my brother's. They wanted it and they made sure they got it." His eyes were bloodshot. I'd always assumed that Grant had gone bankrupt before he'd died, and that was why the marina ended up being taken over by the town. Paul obviously felt that things hadn't worked out fairly, whatever had gone on. "So what are you here for? You got an anchor for me, too?"

For a moment, I wasn't sure I'd heard him right. I wanted to ask him to repeat himself. But the rage radiating off him made me change tactics instead. "Well, it's not so much the business I wanted to ask about. For my report, I want to write about notable women from the island. I've been reading about your niece, Bess Linsky and—"

Now he lunged toward me, yelling. His words were garbled and furious and the only thing I could decipher was "Get out!"

In a panic, I backed away as fast as I could, through the jangling glass door and past the stacks of fishing rods and lures. Paul kept coming. My bike was about fifteen yards behind me, on the dock. I could turn and run, I thought. He was in bad shape, and I was probably faster. But I was too scared to turn my back on him. I felt my way backward, one hand guiding me along the railing that edged the water. I took big, awkward steps, keeping my eyes on him but picturing in my mind how much farther it would be to my bike. Damn. Why hadn't I parked it facing the road? Now I would have to turn it around before I could get out. It was stupid to come out here alone, at night, without telling anyone where I was. On the other hand, why should I have been worried? Stone Cove Island was safe. Nothing bad ever happened here. Or, almost nothing.

Paul was getting closer. He was ranting less in favor of moving faster, which seemed to take some effort through his beer haze. Every few steps, he would lose balance and I would make up a little ground. It was three, big, backward steps, I guessed, maybe four, until I got to my bike. If I went any faster I might overshoot the end of the railing and end up in the water. When I got to the place the railing stopped, I kept my hand reached out behind me and made my steps very straight. Three, two. On one, I hoped I would collide with the metal handlebars and not the bay. Instead, I collided with something else. It was a someone actually. He grabbed my arm. Paul pulled up short, startled. I turned around, now even more terrified, and saw Charlie.

"Come on," Charlie hissed. "Get out of here."

Instantly we turned and ran, leaving my bike behind and Paul staring after us. I looked back once to see if he would follow, but he didn't. I thought of a junkyard dog, running only the length his chain would allow him to go.

We ran as far as we could, which was almost to the lighthouse. We sat down on the rock just outside. I was gasping for air.

"Charlie, what are you doing out here?" I panted.

His lungs were heaving, his eyes wild as Paul's, but clear. "I think you mean, what are you doing out here? And thank you for showing up when you did?"

"Yes," I said. "Both of those. Thank you."

He straightened, catching his breath. He avoided my gaze, glancing back toward the dock. "I felt bad about the library today. I wanted to explain. I came to your house, but you were just leaving on your bike. So I ran after you."

"You ran here? It's three miles." The deer and raccoon sounds were now making sense.

"Yeah," he said. "It's a pretty long run. What were you doing at the marina at night?"

I wanted to tell him the whole story. There were so many pieces he'd missed, I had to think where to start. It felt like a big jumble.

"Well," I said, "the first thing is, I found my mom's diary from when she was in high school. But that's not why I'm out here. I can tell you more about the diary later." I hesitated, then added, "If you're interested."

"I'm interested," he said.

"When I was at the library today, I was looking up the stuff I told you about. I found it in the *Providence Journal.* The three people who found Bess's things after the murder. One was Billy Landron. You remember the Landrons? They moved to London?"

He nodded.

"Another was Paul. Bess's uncle. He was out surfing when Billy found her clothes and hair in the lighthouse. I thought I could ask him to tell me about it, but when I got there, he was drunk and, um, unfriendly. I should have left right away. He was angry when I asked about his family and the marina, and then when I mentioned Bess's name, he completely freaked out. I don't know what would have happened if you hadn't been there."

"Me either," Charlie said, looking serious. "Do you think he killed Bess?"

I shuddered. "I kind of do now."

"Who was the third person? At the lighthouse?"

I hesitated again. "I'm really not sure whether I should tell you."

"Why? Of course tell me," he said.

"Okay. If you're sure you want to know. It was your dad."

Charlie took this in, looking stunned.

"He's never talked to you about Bess or any of this, has he?"

"No. He hasn't." Charlie shook his head, his jaw tight.

"He took Bess to the Spring Fling before that summer," I went on, even less sure about telling him this part. "Your mom was really upset about it."

Charlie sat there, very quietly not reacting. It was too much, too uncomfortable. I had to find a way to get off the topic.

"You said you came over to explain something?" I asked. I was nervous to hear what he had been going to say, but anything was better than watching him process what I'd just told him.

"Yeah," he said. "But it's also an 'I'm not sure whether I should tell you.'" He had a girlfriend in Boston, I realized suddenly. That's what this is about.

"Okay," he began. "First of all, I'm sorry about this afternoon. I handled it really badly."

"It's a side of you I wasn't familiar with," I said in a tone I hoped sounded detached.

"So I'm just going to tell you the whole thing, how it happened. And I hope I'm doing the right thing." He looked at me for confirmation, which was hard for me to give since I had no idea what he was about to say.

"After you left the other day—when my mom came in?"

I laughed. "Yes, I remember that part." It's not like I needed my memory jogged.

He laughed too. "My mom said she wanted to talk to me. She'd heard—I guess she was standing there for a while—she'd heard us talking about Bess. She told me she was really worried about me digging up the past. She said she understood about me wanting to be a journalist, but that it was a bad idea for me to be talking about any of this stuff with you."

"Me specifically?" I asked.

"She told me that she'd known your mom really well in high school and that she'd had some serious problems with depression." He looked at me, to see if this road was okay to continue down. I nodded. It's not like this was exactly news to me. "She said after Bess died, your mom was in a really bad state. She said it got so bad your mom had to be hospitalized. She tried to kill herself." Charlie looked at me to see if he was still on familiar ground. He wasn't. But

I wanted him to go on. "So after, she recovered, I guess. Your dad helped get her through it and they ended up getting married. But my mom said she's worried that if all this gets dredged up again, if your mom starts fixating on what happened, that she could get sick again."

My mother had tried to kill herself? I took this in. I hadn't actually thought I was endangering Mom, despite what my father had said. I thought he was just worried about upsetting her and even then mostly because of what a pain she could be. But then I thought about Cat, the Cat of Mom's diary, and her games. Why was she saying this? Why was she so concerned about my mother suddenly, when it was obvious how much they disliked each other? I had no idea what to believe. Charlie was looking at me like he was afraid he'd inflicted serious damage. I wanted to reassure him. And change the subject.

"Oh, is that all?" I said, trying to make my voice light. "I thought you just didn't want to kiss me."

His head shot up, his eyes locking with mine. His lips curled in a puzzled smile. "Are you serious?" he whispered.

"Very," I said. Before he could respond, I stepped forward and pressed my lips against his.

Maybe this was only "apocalyptic energy"; maybe whatever flame had sparked so suddenly between Charlie Pender and me would die the second things returned to normal on the island. On the other hand, maybe things would never return to normal ever again. And right now, that didn't scare me so much.

IT FELT LIKE THE longest day of my life but by the time Charlie and I walked back it was only eight o'clock. I was worried I would never see my bike again. I could see Paul in his fury dumping it right in the bay. It turned out that while Charlie had been taking a break from me, he had not taken a break from Bess. He'd spent time at the library too, trying to find any mention of the Black Anchor Society. He'd come up empty though, both in Internet searches and local history books. Mary Ellen and Cathy, the librarians, didn't know anything about it. We talked the whole way back, piecing together what we each had gathered on our own. Charlie wanted to see the diary, so when we got to my house, I signaled for him to follow me to the shed. The gravel crunched thunderously under our feet, though we were trying to be quiet. Why didn't it make noise in the daytime? I flipped the light and showed Charlie in, handing him the diary.

"Here," I said. "You catch up. I'm just going to duck my head in and tell my parents I'm back so they aren't out looking for me. Maybe there's something about Paul in there." I didn't know if my mom even knew Paul. After tonight, I hoped she didn't.

The back door swung in with a creak. I balanced on the threshold on the arches of my sneakers.

"Mom?" I called. She came from the kitchen, a light dusting of flour on her sleeves. "I have to run to Meredith's for a sec to get a book."

"Eliza, it's a school night." She pursed her lips. I smelled pumpkin bread.

"Mom, the book's for school." It was easy to work up exasperation, even for a lie.

"All right. Don't be late."

"Is Dad home?" I let my book bag drop to the floor.

"No, he had another council meeting. Preservation review again."

"You didn't go?"

She shrugged. "He'll be home in an hour or so. He didn't think it would go too late." Charlie and I had an hour. I walked through the house to the front, left that way and then backtracked to the shed. Charlie was deep in the diary. He barely heard me come in.

"Nothing about Paul so far," he said. "But . . . wow. It's unbelievable. It's like they were all different people back then."

"I wonder," I said. "If my mom's still like that underneath and just better at hiding it."

"It must be hard to read," he said.

"It's . . . yeah. Upsetting. But I knew some of it. Not the part you told me. But she's still up and down. Like in the diary."

"My mom comes off as so, I don't know what. Venal."

"Well, yes, but that's according to my seventeen-year-old mom. You have to take it with a pretty big grain of salt when you consider the source." Actually, I thought his mom seemed just as described in the diary, but you couldn't say that to someone about his own mother. "It's clear she was into your dad though. She definitely knew what she wanted."

"That part sounds like her. I think we should look at the section right before Bess's murder, or what was going on with any of them back then. Maybe she mentions a guy Bess met that summer? Or anything strange?"

"Sure. I haven't read the whole thing." The diary was thick and crammed with my mom's tiny, swirly writing. Pages had words along the margin where she'd run out of space and turned up the side of the page, and little observations added later, crammed in above or below what she'd already written. It gave the book a feverish quality. I sat down on the floor beside him. He was wearing a flannel shirt and it was warm against my shoulder.

"Are you cold?" he asked, reading my mind.

"I'm okay. I didn't bring anything to write with though. We might want to take notes." My dad usually had a Sharpie or a carpenter's pencil lying around in his woodshop. I started to open drawers. Charlie skimmed the August pages.

"So here's what was going on before Bess died in August," he began. "My mom was mad that Dad hung out with Bess at a party. Some girl named Lynn cut her hair just like Mom's and all three of them made fun of her. Mom wanted Willa to tell Bess to stay away from Jimmy, but Willa said no—"

"Willa said no? My God. Red-letter day." I was still digging around, looking for something to write with. My fingers brushed a rough piece of metal.

"My mom is so mad at everyone all the time in this. Is that what girls are really like?"

"Some girls, I guess." I reached back farther, feeling for the metal object. It seemed too big and too heavy to be a pen. I grasped what felt like a ring on one end and pulled it from the drawer.

"Charlie," I gasped.

I was holding a black anchor.

TEN

Charlie came over to stand with me at the worktable where I had laid down the anchor. We both stared at it. *Gobsmacked* was the word that leaped to mind for some reason. Theo Dorset, on the British Olympic sailing team, always says it. I don't think we have an equivalent term, but I certainly had the equivalent feeling. I felt sick, really.

The anchor was made of iron, about four inches long and heavy for its size. It had a ring on one end. You could tie a thin rope to it or wear it as a necklace. Although, picturing the latter, it would be like wearing a metal albatross or brand. I thought back to tenth-grade English, Hester Prynne in *The Scarlet Letter*. She had been banished within her own village, forced to wear the scarlet *A* and parade her shame as she went about her daily activities. I would have left, if it had been me, but it probably wasn't so easy to do that as a young, pregnant woman back then. Or now, come to think of it.

"It couldn't be a real anchor of some kind, could it?" asked Charlie. He already knew the answer to that.

"Maybe for a sailboat in your bathtub," I answered. "Why does my dad have it?" I went to put the anchor back where I'd found it.

"And who's it for?" he asked. He got out his phone and snapped a picture. "Okay. We better put it back where we found it."

I put the anchor back exactly as I had discovered it, or close enough I hoped. The blood was pounding in my ears.

"I don't know what to do now," I said.

"We need to figure out where it came from and figure out what your dad is planning to do with it."

"My dad would never hurt anyone," I said.

"I know," said Charlie. "We'll figure out what it means. Don't worry." He leaned toward me and kissed my forehead, then circled his arms around me. In just a few days it felt like I'd gone from trusting the whole island to trusting just one person. All of a sudden, I felt scared. I didn't like change. I'd been lying to myself when I'd kissed him earlier. I liked the way things had been before, Charlie notwithstanding. Of course, Charlie was a big notwithstanding.

IT WAS VERY HARD to sleep. Charlie had lingered in the backyard with me, our heads and hands together, until I got too nervous that my mom would look out the window or my dad would find us outside. I lay in bed, staring at the water marks on the ceiling left by the storm. I was shocked by the anchor, shocked that it was even possible that the myth about the island could be true, but I could not believe my dad was part of it: my dad, who had lived here his whole life, who had built and repaired so many homes here, who had spent so many hours coaching swimming just because he loved it, who had patiently nursed my mom through so many dark spells.

Could he really be the one to deliver the threatening anchor? The one to decide who got to stay and who had to go from Stone Cove? I did not think it was in his nature, that kind of judgmental outlook on the world, deciding who belonged and who didn't. He liked to be part of the gang, a friend to everyone. There had to be some other explanation. I rolled over for the thousandth time, trying to get comfortable. At last, just as I started to drift off, my body jolted back awake, as though I'd caught myself falling. My father who loved swimming, who was a great swimmer. My mother never had been. Bess was an excellent swimmer, and so was Dad.

IN THE MORNING WHEN I woke up, my eyes felt like they'd been rubbed with sandpaper. My stomach churned. I'd forgotten to eat dinner, but food was the last thing I wanted. I wasn't sick really, I knew. But I couldn't go to school. I couldn't fake my way through a whole day instead of finding out what that black anchor was doing in my dad's shop. I lay in bed, trying to come up with a plan. I didn't think Dad would leave something like that lying around for long, even in what was supposed to be his private domain. It seemed too risky. But I couldn't follow him around the island all day.

I went into the bathroom, ran the hot water in the sink

and threw a towel over my head and let the steam envelop me. Luckily the power was on, so there was hot water. Then I dried my face and stumbled to the kitchen. It wasn't hard to look exhausted.

"Mom," I said in a scratchy voice that I hoped I wasn't overdoing. "I don't feel well." She put her hand to my forehead and tensed her own with worry.

"You feel hot. Do you want to go back to bed?"

"But I have school . . ." I said, my voice wispy.

"Better to get well. Missing one day won't hurt you."

I nodded. "Where's Dad?" I asked.

"At the inn. They're starting on the roof today. Finally." If my dad was at the inn, Charlie would be able to keep tabs on the anchor.

"Are you going to be here?"

"I have to go to market this morning but I shouldn't be long. I can stay home with you," she replied.

"Thanks," I said, even though that wasn't why I was asking. I turned back to my room, got dressed and lay under the covers until I heard her click and bolt the door on her way out. She always locked the door when she left, even if there was still someone at home. Then I counted to one hundred and slipped out the back way.

In the shed, I had the creepy feeling of being watched. *It must be my own guilt,* I thought. The anchor was still in the drawer, exactly as I had left it. That meant my father wasn't delivering it to the Penders, Colleen or any guests at the inn. Maybe, I told myself optimistically, he's not delivering it to anyone.

Back inside, I wrote a quick note to my mom—on paper.

She wasn't much of a text message girl. *Feeling so much better. Going to try school for the afternoon.* I took my book bag, my math notebook and Mom's diary. I was going to the library to see what I could find out about Grant, Paul and what had happened to the marina. I had until about 4 P.M., when my dad would be home from work. I texted Charlie. I wanted him to come to the library with me, but it seemed like a better—less fun, but better—idea for him to stay close to home and see if my dad did anything weird. Charlie texted back that he'd stick around. miss you though. That was nice. ditto, I wrote.

Terminal 3 was open. The library was almost deserted. That meant I could spread out and not feel worried about anyone reading over my shoulder. Once I reassured Mary Ellen that I didn't need help, she went back to her office and left me alone. I thought briefly of my bike. How was I going to get it back? I wasn't in a hurry to return to the marina, that was for sure.

There weren't any news stories about the town taking over the marina. Grant's boating accident didn't even make any paper other than our local one. The *Gazette* ran a short obituary, no picture: Grant Guthy, former owner of the Stone Cove Marina Boatyard and Boat Rentals had drowned in an accident while fishing alone. The vague details and lack of description of Grant himself implied disapproval, which I took to mean either drinking or drugs. Neither Karen nor Bess was mentioned.

Counting backward, I figured Bess would have been about eleven at the time. I wondered if my mom was already friends with her when her father died. My searches on Paul turned up two DUIs in the *Gazette* crime blotter. *Maybe he could use my bike,* I thought. In the issue before Grant's death there was an ad for the Marina Boatyard (UNDER NEW MANAGEMENT!) but no article.

The transfer seemed to have taken place silently. Had Grant lost the business through debt? Or had he made a lot of money selling it? If that were true, would Bess have inherited the money? Could she have been killed for that reason? What if Paul thought that the money belonged to him? I didn't know who would be able to answer these questions, but this part of the story felt more like gossip than fact, so I decided to take my coffee break at the Picnic Basket rather than talking to Jay.

NANCY WAS WORKING ALONE when I arrived. I poured myself a cup of the strong blend from the self-service urns they had out, then spent a long time fussing with the cream and sugar to give us more time to talk.

"You know what's funny?" I said. I couldn't think of a subtle way to start the conversation, so I went for picking up where we had left off. "I just saw Paul Guthy. You know Bess's uncle?"

"Yeah?" she said uncertainly. I waited for her to offer some commentary, but she was uncharacteristically silent. I went on.

"Well, it turns out—you know how Greg said surfers discovered Bess's clothes after she drowned?—Paul was one of the surfers."

"I guess I do remember that," said Nancy.

"Did he work at the marina then? I was wondering if

he'd worked there since Grant died. Taking over for his brother."

"That's more recent. Back then he worked for us. He was between things, and Greg liked to help him out."

"Really? He worked for you around the time Bess drowned?"

"I know he did. He worked the summer fair booth with me the night it happened. I remember thinking afterward how strange it was, everyone in town having fun while that was going on. That's why I'm sure it wasn't anyone from here."

The summer fair was an annual carnival that took place on the green. All the local shops set up booths and there were games and live music. It was funny I hadn't put together that that had taken place the same night. My mom hadn't mentioned it in her diary. It was true that the whole island usually did show up for the fair, but I knew that Bess and at least some of her friends had been at The Slip later that night. Mom had mentioned Dad and Jimmy. Was Cat there? The fair ended with a midnight fireworks show. If Paul had worked the Picnic Basket's booth, he would have stayed for cleanup after that. Nancy couldn't have moved everything herself. So he couldn't have been at the lighthouse that night.

"Oh," I said. "So he wasn't involved with the marina after the town took over?" I was interrupted by the sound of Greg clearing his throat. Nancy turned and looked like a startled deer. Greg gave her a stern look, and her nervous expression turned to guilt.

"I should get back to work, Eliza. Can I get you anything else?"

"No thanks. Hi, Greg," I said, super friendly, then slipped out to let them work out whatever domestic squabble was going to ensue. Last time I'd been there, he'd warned her not to talk so much. This time he didn't want her talking, and she knew it.

BACK AT THE LIBRARY, I was stuck. Paul had seemed like the obvious choice, but now he had an alibi. I went back to searching old issues of the *Gazette*, but kind of aimlessly. Drowning, I realized, made the truth especially difficult to determine. It wasn't like a shooting or stabbing. It seemed almost impossible to know exactly what happened, when and how. There had been so many famous, unsolved cases: the actress Natalie Wood, or that architect in the Hamptons. He'd left his clothes behind on the beach as well. Or the singer Jeff Buckley, walking right into the Mississippi River.

BESS HAD NOT COMMITTED suicide, I reminded myself. Her hair had been cut off. Her clothes were covered in blood. I typed in "drowning" in the *Gazette* archive search, not expecting anything to come up.

I'd made only a few quick notes before a text from Charlie interrupted me. your dad just left. call me when you are alone. need to talk.

I'd lost track of time. My dad would get home before me now unless I ran. I wished for the third time that I hadn't left my bike. I made it home in a half-run, half-awkward speed walk, my book bag banging the outside of my thigh painfully. No one was home. That either meant

I'd beat my dad there or already missed him. I hurried to the shed and opened the drawer. Then I called Charlie.

"The anchor is gone," I said before he'd even said hello. *That was a dumb move,* I thought immediately. If this had been a movie, the killer would have answered instead of Charlie.

"I'm glad you called," said Charlie. He sounded out of breath, a little off balance. "Some weird stuff happened today. I was outside cleaning paint brushes. I heard my dad and your dad talking. My dad said not to worry, now Malloy wouldn't be a problem. He just needed a reminder."

"A reminder?"

The word caught in my throat. My dad was taking the anchor to school. Malloy would still be there. Charlie was silent. A hundred thoughts seemed to zip back and forth between us, ricocheting through the cell-o-sphere. I wanted to say, *Oh no. Not your dad too.* And, *How could we not know our own parents?* And, *What's going to happen to us, now that everything we thought we could believe in is ruined?* I thought Charlie probably wanted to say these things to me too, but he didn't.

"You should get over to school," he said instead. "Want me to meet you there?"

"No," I said. "If I go, I can pretend I needed help with something in English. If you're there it'll seem weird. Meet me at the diner though. I have some other stuff I need to tell you."

I hung up and then I was running again, running and cursing Paul Guthy and hoping I wasn't too late.

ELEVEN

It was strangely quiet at the school, considering there were still families camped out in the gym and classes had ended only an hour or two earlier. I'd run so fast I almost bumped right into my dad, who was just walking through the front doors when I arrived. I wasn't sure what tack to take: intercept him before he got to Mr. Malloy or follow him to see what he planned to do, then barge in, making it look like a coincidence that we were both there at the same time. I lingered, thinking, behind some evergreens that hadn't lost their needles in the storm. Because I still couldn't really believe my dad could be part of anything deceitful like this, I decided to follow him. Unfortunately, I timed it wrong. When I entered the hall, my dad was nowhere in sight.

I was forced to head straight for Malloy's office. I hurried up the north stairs to the second floor. When I got to the office, I knocked and swung the door open all at once. Malloy was alone, grading papers and extremely surprised to see me.

"Eliza," he said, and waited for my explanation.

"Hi, Mr. Malloy," I said. "You haven't seen my dad, have you?"

"Your father?" He blinked in apparent confusion, his forehead creased.

"Oh, I thought I saw him on my way in. But maybe I made a mistake." If my dad wasn't here yet, then I would need to keep Malloy talking until he arrived.

"The other day . . ." I began, not really knowing where I was going. "The other day you mentioned what a great writer Bess Linsky was." He looked completely blank. I hadn't imagined that, had I? He didn't say anything, so I forged ahead.

"I'd be really interested to read that paper she wrote. The example you said you used in European lit?"

"I have no idea where that would be, if I still even have it. I haven't taught that class in a long time. With all the testing we're required to do, the curriculum has become much more . . . focused."

"Oh," I said. I had nowhere to go from here.

"You weren't in class today."

Damn. I'd forgotten I'd be busting myself by showing up at school. That had been stupid.

"I know," I said. "My mom is going to write me a note." *Keep it vague,* I told myself.

"Eliza, I don't know what has inspired your interest in Bess, but I'm not sure it's healthy. We are all under tremendous stress since the hurricane. I wonder if this . . . *obsession,* not to put too fine a point on it . . . is a reaction on your part to the recent events here."

"Did someone tell you to say that to me?" I asked, point-blank. I was fed up with being kept in the dark.

"What do you mean by that?" he asked me. His eyes narrowed and I didn't know if he was thinking I was paranoid or if he thought I was somehow threatening him. I swallowed, imagining him thinking: *The apple doesn't fall far from the tree.*

"Nothing," I said. "People just don't like to talk about Bess, and I don't understand why." He nodded but didn't say anything. "I should go."

If my dad were coming here, he would have arrived by now. I left Malloy's office and closed the door behind me. I stepped to the side so he wouldn't see me through the glass door and timed ten minutes on my phone. I waited, leaning against the chilly wall, for Dad to show up. When he didn't, I smiled to myself. Charlie and I could be wrong about all of this. There were lots of possible explanations.

As I left the school, my dad was the one to spot me.

"Eliza," he called across the lawn. "Feeling better?" I joined him, and he hugged me around the shoulders with one arm. I noticed he was in jeans and a sweater and he carried nothing with him. The anchor was four inches long. It wouldn't fit in a pocket without being visible.

"I had a meeting with my English teacher," I lied. Dad didn't react at all. "What about you?"

"Swim coach meeting," he said.

I sighed with a shaky smile. In the chaos since the storm, in the whirlwind of Charlie and everything else, I'd almost lost track of the days of the week. Today was Thursday. He had a swim team meeting every other Thursday. I hadn't thought of that. I hugged him back. There was a reasonable explanation after all. "Where are you headed?"

"The diner," I said. "Meeting Charlie."

He flashed me an unreadable look.

"What?"

"Nothing," he said, his lopsided smile taking over. "It's nice to have him back on the island, isn't it? He's a good kid."

WHEN I GOT TO the diner, to my surprise, Charlie wasn't there. I found a booth and sat alone, opening Mom's diary at random. Mom and Bess had taken a day trip to Salem— research, Bess said, for her part in the play *The Crucible*. Bess was obsessed with the history about the witch trials. She led Mom from place to place, pointing out where the real Goody Proctor had lived, the Witch House where Judge Corwin lived, and the house where Nathaniel Hawthorne had written *The Scarlet Letter*. Mom, who, I imagined, was too shy for theater, was along for the ride. The two of them, wandering the crooked narrow streets, pigging out on fudge from a tourist shop, talking about everything under the sun.

"Nice to be away from Misery Island," Bess joked. I could see my mom smiling. It was the first passage I'd read where my mom seemed to feel free. *She was happy that day,* I thought, something I realized I couldn't picture for myself. Had I ever really seen her that way? I skipped ahead to an entry from May, right after the Spring Fling:

Bess made me throw up. She said it was the best thing to do. She stood above me, holding my hair back in a damp knot against

*my head. Like she was a grown-up, like a mother. I could feel how
clammy and sweaty the back of my neck was. I was disgusting. The
strands of hair near my face smelled like vomit. I was ashamed to
have her so close. Bess didn't care.*

I told her I was sorry.

*She said, I know. Tonight it feels like it's all too much. Tomorrow
you'll be yourself again. You just have to look ahead to tomorrow.
Imagine you're already there and this feeling is behind you.*

*I believed her, the way she said that. I thanked her four times,
and I made her promise not to tell anyone, and she made me
promise that I'd call her the next time I felt this way. I said there
wouldn't be a next time, but she made me promise, anyway.*

She said that tomorrow, it will be better.

*I hoped she was right. She helped me lie down on the floor. She
zipped the sleeping bag up for me. Then she lay down on her own
bed, right above me. I closed my eyes. The room spun. Tomorrow,
it will be better.*

Wow. My mom, drunk. My dad was right, I thought. It
seemed like Bess had been a good friend to her. I wondered what she'd been up to that night, to end up in that
state. I reread the entry to see if my mom mentioned a
party or bar. *She made me promise I'd call her the next time I felt
this way.* Had I read it wrong? Had my mom been drunk?
Or was her suicide attempt after Bess's death not her first?
Was it possible I really was endangering Mom by delving
into her unstable past?

I didn't even hear Charlie come in. When I looked up
next, he was sitting across from me. For a minute, those
gold-flecked brown eyes tugged me from the grim place
I'd been visiting in my mind. Then I saw that he looked

equally shaken. His dad was "taking care of things" with Malloy, whatever that meant. My dad and Jimmy, talking behind closed doors, planning something. I felt like my life was a puppet show where the curtains had been thrown back and suddenly you could see all the wires being pulled behind the stage.

"So, hi," I said.

"So, hi. Did you make it to school before your dad?"

"Not exactly. He was on his way in when I got there. He didn't go to see Mr. Malloy though. He was at a swim team meeting." Even to me my smile felt forced.

"Did he see you?"

"Not until afterward," I said. "He didn't have the anchor with him. I don't know what happened. Could we have been wrong about all of this?"

"What were they talking about then, giving Malloy a reminder?"

I shrugged. "Maybe he got the message on his own. He wouldn't talk to me about Bess, pretended he'd never said anything about her. Told me I was developing an unhealthy obsession."

"You probably are," Charlie joked. "And so am I." We both laughed and I turned away, feeling suddenly shy. Were we still talking about Bess?

Kelly set two paper place mats, showing a cartoon map of the states with a giant lobster looming over New England, down in front of us. So far, I had only ordered coffee.

"You need menus?" she asked.

Charlie shook his head. "You hungry?" he asked me. "You want to share some fries?"

I nodded. Kelly disappeared to the kitchen. Charlie traced the lobster on the placemat with one finger. I pointed to Chicago, illustrated with a cluster of tall buildings surrounded by cornfields.

"Do you like corn?" I said. "I wish we had some crayons. We could color these in." In Texas, there was a bull with a big star on his forehead.

"Where do you want to go?" Charlie asked. "For college, I mean."

"I don't know," I said. "I'll probably stay in state. Or in New England, at least. UMass, or maybe UNH."

He laughed. "That'd be some serious culture shock," he teased. University of New Hampshire was less than two hours away. "Don't you want to get out and see the world a little? Or at least the country? You can always come back."

"I don't know," I said. "I'm happy here. I'm not in a rush to get out. I'm not saying you shouldn't. I just haven't felt the need."

"How do you know what you're missing if you never even look around?" he asked.

I shrugged. "I know people think college is everything, but I don't. I mean, I'll go. It's not that I don't think it's important, but I think you can get a good education anywhere."

"But it's not just the courses," he argued. "It's the people around you, the place, the culture, new ideas, the stuff you didn't expect before you got there."

I returned his gaze. "How do you know? You haven't gone yet."

"I don't," he said. "But I can hope, right?"

I nodded.

"Listen, do one thing for me."

"What?" I asked.

"Close your eyes and pick a spot on the map. Apply to one school in that place, wherever you land. You don't have to go if you get in. Just . . . give yourself the option, in case you change your mind."

"Are you serious?" I smiled.

"Why not? You can pick a common app school. It won't be any extra work."

"Okay," I said. "Why not?" I closed my eyes and spiraled my finger above the table. I half hoped to land on Chicago. Thoughts of how little time was left before Charlie went away were already starting to pop into my brain with annoying frequency. *Lame,* I told myself. You are not going to follow your boyfriend to college. Then I had to correct myself: Charlie wasn't even really my boyfriend.

"Am I still over the map?" I asked, still circling my finger at random.

"Yup. Come on. Stop procrastinating and pick a spot."

"Okay." I veered in the direction I thought was west. "Maybe I'll go for Hawaii. Another island might feel like home." I put my finger down and opened my eyes.

"All right," said Charlie. "Looks like you're going to UCLA. Or USC. Congratulations."

I wrinkled my nose. "USC is too expensive. Ugly school colors. And, the Trojans?"

"I see your point. UCLA it is."

"You're crazy," I told him.

"You have to apply. You promised."

"Fine. I'll check the UCLA box, okay? Are you happy now?"

"I am, actually." He returned my smile, but then his expression turned serious. "What do you think our dads are really up to?"

"I don't know," I said. "I'm kind of afraid to find out."

He nodded. "You said you found out something else that you wanted to tell me."

"Yeah. After last night, I was convinced Paul was the only likely . . . killer? That sounds so weird to say about a person you know. But it turns out Paul used to work for the Picnic Basket back then. The night Bess drowned was the night of the summer fair. Paul was there working until at least midnight and probably way later. Most of the island would have been there."

"That's good for the random tourist or serial killer theory. Although, looking at Jay's notes, there wasn't anything to back up the idea of a serial killer. Unless Bess was the first victim and then the guy retired prematurely. Sorry, I don't mean to make jokes. I don't really know how to talk about this."

I nodded. "But from my mom's diary, we know that Bess showed my mom the letter. Why would a random stranger write her a letter before he killed her? Why would he say she knew why she deserved to die? And any number of people could have left the fair in time to be at the lighthouse when Bess left the bar. We know my dad and your dad and maybe your mom all went to The Slip that night, maybe late if they also went to the fair, but the bars are only open till, what, one A.M.? Who else was there with them?"

And where had my mother been? I thought, but I didn't say it out loud. Everyone knew that saying you were home alone was the world's worst alibi, at least on TV cop shows.

"Bess left before any of them. And she was alone," said Charlie, piecing together the timeline.

"We think. Or, my mom thinks. So, after I talked to Nancy I went back to the library and I felt stuck. I thought about drownings and how it's particularly hard to know what really happened, especially if the body's never found. I started Googling drownings on Stone Cove Island in the *Gazette* archives. We've had a lot of drownings here. Did you know that?"

"We are on an island," Charlie pointed out. "Water on every side."

"Right," I said. "I realize that. That's not what's weird about it. I'll give you an example. There was a developer from Florida who bought land here in the eighties. He wanted to build a big condo development and resort. The island's review boards fought him and eventually won. Then he decided what the island really needed was a causeway from Rockport. Can you imagine?" Charlie nodded. Something like that would change everything about Stone Cove. We sat silent a moment, both picturing Miami along East Beach.

"Yeah. That would have been crazy. How did they stop it?"

"They couldn't. They took him to court, but for whatever reason, maybe he was really hooked up with the state politicians, they approved the initial plan and were going to put it on the ballot in the next election to fund it."

"Something must have stopped it though."

"Not it," I said. "Him. He drowned in a swimming accident a month after the state approved his plan. He was the main force behind it, so the idea kind of just went away. Another example: there was this African American family who moved here. The dad wanted to join the Anchor Club. Same era. Before he could be initiated, he and his wife drove their car off the road near the bluff and drowned."

"How did you figure out that those were connected?"

"Working backward. Finding out who drowned and then looking for news stories related to them right before. This guy would have been the first black member in the late seventies. The next black member joined in 1998."

"You think they were sent anchors before they drowned."

I shrugged. "None of the stories mentioned that. Of course."

"No one could ever prove that those weren't just accidents though."

"Exactly. And no one can prove who killed Bess or why. But in each case, the problem goes away."

"What kind of problem was Bess?"

"That's what we have to figure out. She could have been a different problem for different people. Maybe she knew someone's secret. Maybe she saw something she wasn't supposed to. Maybe it was about money."

"Right," he said. He stared down at the table, thinking. "Maybe—"

A gruff throat-clearing interrupted us. Officer Bailey stood next to our table looking like she wanted to join us.

"Hi, kids," she said cheerfully. "Eliza. I've been hoping

to catch up with you." The letter. I knew she'd corner me eventually.

"Should I go?" asked Charlie.

"Oh, no. No need," she said. "I just have a few questions. Just trying to check some details."

"Would you like to sit down?" I asked, not really meaning it. I wanted to stay here in my little bubble with Charlie, disturbed only by the occasional coffee refill. But I was going to have to talk to her sooner or later. And maybe I could find out something from her. Was she reopening Bess's case? Had she worked on the murder when it had happened? Or would she have been too young back then? It was hard to tell. She had one of those faces you could picture looking the same at every age, fifteen or fifty.

She sat, nodding to Kelly to come over.

"Earl Grey with milk," she told her, then turned her attention on me. "So. Your father filled me in a little, but I'd like to hear the story in your words." The story? Did she know Charlie and I had been playing amateur detective? I must have looked blank, because she went on. "How you found the letter?"

"Oh, right," I began. "Well, it was on the cleanup day at the lighthouse. When I went upstairs. The keeper's office was a mess, with papers blown everywhere. I picked the letter up. Maybe it stood out because of the blue paper."

"Who else was at the lighthouse that day?"

"Meredith and Colleen. But they were downstairs."

"And then what did you do with the letter?"

"I took it home and showed my parents."

Officer Bailey nodded, pulling a notepad and pen from

her thick belt. "My dad thought we should give it to you. I would have given it to you right away, but I wasn't sure you'd think it was important."

"Not a problem," she said. "Well, thanks for your help."

"Wait, that's it?" I said.

"Yup."

"Well, does this mean you'll reopen the investigation?"

"If the letter turns out to be authentic, which I think is pretty darn unlikely. But that'll be for the state police to decide. We don't investigate homicides locally, you know."

I frowned. "Of course it's authentic. Why would you say it's not authentic? I know it is."

Officer Bailey's eyed me skeptically. "You know it is? Now why would you say that?"

I opened my mouth to speak and then closed it again. The reason I knew was because my mother had quoted it in her diary. She was the only one besides Bess who had read the letter. If I told Officer Bailey about the diary, I would drag my mom into it. Or worse, I would implicate her.

"It . . . I don't know. But who else would write something like that? And the paper looked old." My backtracking was pathetic, but I couldn't think of what else to say. Charlie put a hand on my shoulder.

"Eliza's pretty shook up about being the one to find it," Charlie said.

Luckily Officer Bailey seemed to buy his excuse for me. Her features settled back into the sympathetic pose she'd started with. "I'm sure it was a little shock for you, Eliza. But it's nothing to get worked up about. It's most likely just a prank. Kids. It's getting close to Halloween. But the state police will check it out and see if there's anything to it. Anyway, thanks for your help. Hello to your folks from me, okay?" She stood up to go.

"That's all?" I asked.

"That's all I need."

"Well, is this the first time . . . I mean, did you work on the investigation originally?" I was risking insulting her, but I couldn't help it. I had to ask.

She laughed. "Dear God, no! I was a kid then too. Same class as Bess Linsky."

"Oh. Ha," I laughed weakly. "Of course." It seemed like everyone on the island had graduated that year. The door of the diner swung partway open with a jingle. The deputy sheriff stuck his head in the door.

"Lynn," he said. "When you get a minute. On the radio." He gestured toward their squad car with his thumb.

"Be right there."

Lynn. I'd forgotten that was Officer Bailey's name, if I'd ever known it. Lynn. *LB.* The girl who tagged along at the spring fling. The girl who copied Cat's hairstyle and was laughed at. The girl who'd wanted so desperately to be included. How had Bess treated her back then? If only I had Bess's diary instead of my mom's. I so longed to know what had been going on in her head that summer. Or maybe I just wanted to leave my mother's head behind.

CHARLIE AND I WERE halfway to the green when I realized I'd forgotten my book bag at the diner. I hurried back. The place had cleared out. It was the lull between afternoon pie and early dinner, and Kelly was alone, wiping down tables. I found my bag right where I'd left it, on the banquette in the booth. I held it up to Kelly and rolled my eyes to say "I'm a complete idiot."

She smiled as if she agreed. "No problem, Eliza."

WE WERE QUIET AT dinner. Dad, usually the chattiest of the three of us, seemed far away. I'd snuck out to the shed when I'd come home and found the anchor back in its hiding place at the back of the drawer. I wondered what that could mean. My mother was focused on carefully dividing the food on her plate. It was an unconscious habit. She would separate it into piles like a little kid, not wanting the different foods to touch. From time to time she would look up at me or Dad and ask a question. I often had the impression she needed to remind herself to do this. Keep talking. Stay in the world.

"How was school?"

I almost said I hadn't gone, but caught myself. "In the afternoon? It was okay."

"You feeling better?"

"Yes."

She pushed the roasted carrots to one side, lining them up and then said to my dad, "Everything going well with the roof?"

My dad scowled. "Jimmy's causing hassles with the board. I don't know what's going to happen."

I could see Mom's nerves bristle at this, hackles rising on a cat. "But it will be okay, right? You and Jimmy always work things out. You don't want to get on the wrong side of him, Nate. He gives you so much business."

"I know that, Willa."

"So, you can work things out," she insisted.

"I'm trying. There's nothing for you to worry about at this point."

She managed to look chastened and pleased at the same time. *My father doesn't like his job*, I realized with a shock. It was the first time I'd ever come to that conclusion, but I could suddenly see clearly that it was true. I wondered if he had imagined his life would be something else.

I helped Mom with the dishes and then she and Dad put a nature program on. I didn't have any homework, but I pretended I did. I went to my room, opened my laptop, and tapped UCLA into the search window. I wouldn't really go. I knew that. But it couldn't hurt to apply, even just as a private joke between me and Charlie. *Nice to be away from Misery Island.* I could almost hear Bess talking to me.

THE CRASH WOKE ME up from a comatose sleep. It took a minute to remember where I was. Then I head my dad, half running, half stumbling to the front door. My alarm clock read 2:45 A.M. I jumped out of bed, pulled on a lumpy cardigan and followed him.

There was no one outside. Down the street a neighbor's dog barked, warning us belatedly. Where was Salty in all this? Probably curled up in a ball at my mom's feet, sleeping right through it. He was getting a little deaf. My father stood at the end of the driveway staring into the darkness, in a T-shirt and bare feet, despite the chill. I wandered slowly out to meet him. Had he told my mom to stay inside? Or was she too afraid to come out?

"Dad?" I said. At his feet lay my mangled bike. Well, that explained the metallic clatter we'd heard. It didn't explain how Paul knew where I lived, which was an uncomfortable feeling. I hadn't really believed him when he said he knew who I was. Or I hadn't wanted to.

"Dad?" I said again. I was standing right next to him, but he was so rigid with anger he couldn't look at me. Now he forced himself to take a deep breath and put a hand on my shoulder.

"Don't worry, kiddo. We'll fix your bike. I'll fix it." He didn't ask what had happened to it, why it was lying twisted in the driveway. "Now go inside. Go back to sleep, okay?"

I nodded. Then I went back into the kitchen and watched through the side window as he walked to the back of the house and stood by the shed. He took out his cell phone. I crawled to the back door, even though the lights were off and he probably couldn't see me. I pushed one of the back windows open, just enough to hear what was going on outside, and sat below it.

"Jimmy, God damn it, Jimmy. That's it. The last straw. I'm done," he was talking into the phone in a whisper, but the rage behind the words carried them hissing across the lawn to me. It was three in the morning. I couldn't believe he was calling Jimmy now. He was supposed to be working things out with him, not ensuring that his project would fall apart. I should have told him in the driveway that it was Paul. But it was too late now. Plus, I told myself in guilty rationalization, he was already fighting with Jimmy. Was it worse for him to think Jimmy had done this than to know I'd gone out to the marina to see Paul? I heard him slam his fist against the side of the shed. I knew I'd better get back to my room before he walked in and caught me eavesdropping.

TWELVE

The next morning, true to his word, Dad was in the shed, my bike turned upside down on a worktable as he untangled the metal. I brought him a cup of black coffee. He was in his pajamas.

"Thanks, kiddo," he said, taking the mug.

"You're not going to work today, Dad?"

"Nope. Taking the day off. Mental health day." I nodded. He could see I was worried.

"It's a good thing. I should have done it long ago. I need some time off." Mom was going to completely freak out. "Go on. You better get ready for school."

"Dad," I ventured. "You had Mr. Malloy for English, right?"

He looked at me with no expression. Or rather, he looked at me, removing any trace of expression from his face. On purpose. Which wasn't the same thing at all.

"I did," he said. "Why do you ask?"

"He's one of my favorite teachers," I said. This was a lie. And Dad knew it. What I meant was: *Please don't hurt Mr.*

Malloy, if you're the one behind the anchor, or if it's someone you know who's planning to do something bad.

"Yeah. He was pretty good as I remember. Hated tardiness, though, am I right?"

"I have English last period, but I take your point, Dad." I turned and headed inside. I had to go to school. I couldn't skip a second day, especially after Malloy had seen me in perfect health. Only right now, school felt like a huge waste of time—the way it had to Bess, all those years ago.

WHEN I ARRIVED WITH only minutes to spare, the perennially early Meredith was on the front steps, talking to Pete Brewer, a dopey jock baseball player in our class. As I joined them, Pete muttered awkwardly, fiddled with his baseball cap and hulked away, making his way into the building, his arms held stiffly away from his body by the overdeveloped muscles along his sides. He reminded me of an ape, although truthfully, he was probably a nice enough guy. The only time I'd heard him talk about anything other than his own stats, however, was in English class, where he wasted tons of time bullshitting about the books he hadn't read. The less he'd read, the longer he rambled.

"What's up?" I said to Meredith, sitting down. She looked a little pained.

"Oh," she said. "Pete just asked me to the Halloween dance."

"Was he bummed you said no?"

"I didn't say no," she said.

"What?" She ignored the question, staring off across the quad, looking miserable. I followed her gaze to the parking lot, where Tim McAllister was just walking up the steps from the parking lot.

"Oh no," I said. "You didn't ask Tim yet."

"No," she said. "Not yet. Who are you going with?"

I loved that about her: thoughtful, even in her darkest moments.

"Charlie," I said without hesitation, though I'd just decided myself. He would go, I thought. He was a nice enough guy to put himself through one night back in high school to make me happy. The idea brought a smile to my lips.

But Meredith barely heard me. Tim was headed straight for us, looking right at Meredith. And looking nervous.

"I should—" I started to get up. Meredith grabbed my wrist, clinging to me for dear life. "Ow!"

"Stay. Please?" I sat back down. Tim slowed, seeing that I'd settled back in, but he was too close to us now to stop without looking like he was turning away.

"Hey, Meredith," he said. "Hey, Eliza." An afterthought, but I was fine with that.

"Hi, Tim!" I said, super friendly, after Meredith let a long, tongue-tied silence elapse.

"I was wondering if you're going to the Halloween dance," he said to Meredith. Poor guy. He was desperate to get it over with. "I mean, if you wanted to go. With me."

Meredith looked miserable. I beat a retreat, making noises about something I needed to turn in before first bell. *Ha,* I said to myself. *I knew he liked her too.* It filled me with a strange happiness, even though my best friend was cringing right now. At least there were still some things on Stone Cove Island I could be certain of. Not everything had changed. For most people, in fact, nothing had changed at all.

THE FOLLOWING WEEK, I was distracted in school, but I was hardly the only one. Kids had lost their schoolbooks and all their homework from the entire fall in the storm. Kids had moved out of their ruined houses and had to improvise pens, paper and backpacks. The computer terminals in the school library had long lines at all times of the day, even with the extended hours that had been added. There were sign-up sheets divided into half-hour blocks. If there were any slots left open, they were usually before 8 A.M. or after 10 P.M. I couldn't imagine writing, say, my paper on "The Individual versus Society in *The Glass Menagerie*" in thirty-minute chunks between 6:00 and 6:30 A.M. Even my teachers seemed dazed. I would sometimes catch Mrs. Russell staring out the window, her thoughts obviously elsewhere, or Mr. Tabersky asking a student to repeat a question he'd missed the first time around.

My dad had fixed my bike. He'd also quit or been fired from Jimmy Pender's restoration job. I wasn't sure which. It was not a topic open for discussion. Mom soldiered on in her nervous way, looking increasingly pinched and jumpy. Occasionally she made noises about going back to substitute teaching or tutoring, which Dad quashed before the words were halfway out of her mouth. The idea of her going back to work seemed to insult him.

Dad's work situation didn't bother me terribly. What bothered me the most during those tense days was that I'd lost Mom's diary.

It wasn't like me at all to lose things. On the other hand, being with Charlie had turned me into not quite my normal self. So I went into Mom-OCD mode. I made mental lists of every place I'd taken it (my house, Dad's shed, Charlie's house, school, the diner, the library, and on and on). I backtracked, trying to remember when I had it last, what I'd been doing, what I'd been thinking about, which part I'd been reading last. I tried to see myself in my memory. Had I placed it in the front or back section of my bag? Had I hidden it on the high shelf of the linen closet or in a drawer in my dresser? Did I leave it under my bed?

In the end, I started to wonder if either of my parents had found it and quietly taken it back. It wasn't in the black bag in Mom's closet—of course I had checked there—but maybe they had found some new, better hiding place. Maybe this was their way of telling me that it was best to keep silent about the past.

THURSDAY AFTERNOON, AS I rode my bike past the grounds of my summer camp on the way to Charlie's, all the campfire songs I'd learned as a kid came back to me in a fractured medley. Round and round in "The Circle Game," and the one about the father who never had time for his son until it was too late; the soldier and the town that fought for a treasure that turned out to just be a stone that said *Peace on Earth*. They were all about a similar regret, I realized: all about not appreciating what you had until you lost it and couldn't get it back.

My dad had done a decent job straightening my wheels, but the front one rubbed in one place so that as it turned it made a metallic moaning sound. I had not been back to the marina, but the rhythmic whine of my bike seemed to bring the marina back to me.

The kitchen at the inn was quiet. The guests who had been stranded by the storm had all gradually found their way back to dry land and no new guests had come to replace them. It was getting close to the slow winter season anyway, but I knew its early arrival this year would stress the Penders and put even more pressure on a successful season next summer. I made my way up the carpeted back stairs.

Oddly, since my dad had fallen out with Jimmy, Charlie's parents had been much nicer to me. I couldn't figure out if they'd just accepted the situation and were making the best of it, or if it was more along the lines of "keep your friends close and your enemies closer."

Charlie and I had planned to be good, by which we meant I would work on my paper and he would work on some short pieces for Jay at *The Gazette*. Ha. We lay on our stomachs on the shaggy white rug in his room. I flipped the pages of *The Glass Menagerie*. Charlie jotted ideas on index cards he spread out around us. If I'm being honest, there was a fair amount of staring into space and staring at each other.

"Oh," I said at one point. "So, I actually did it. I applied to UCLA."

"Are you kidding?" He grinned at me, surprised, and leaned over to kiss me. His lips were soft and tickled a little, where they brushed mine. My scalp tingled along the bottom of my hairline. "We'll see what happens. My test scores are just okay. I'm no Meredith."

"It's hard to imagine anyone saying no to you, Eliza." He kissed me again. We were not going to get any work done. That was clear.

"Like how you couldn't say no to the Halloween dance?" I asked.

"Exactly like that." Charlie laughed. He had agreed to go and even dress up. He was going as Clark Kent. I was going as Katniss Everdeen, from *The Hunger Games*, but I hadn't told him what my costume was going to be. It was going to be a surprise.

"You're a good sport, Charlie."

I yawned, rolled onto my back and stared at the ceiling. It was perfectly white. No cracks. No chips. I could hear the whirr of the space heater in the corner. Flooding had corroded the inn's furnace. It had to be replaced, but it was going to be months before they could get a new one here. I wondered who Jimmy would get to help him with his projects now that my dad was out of the picture. Probably they would patch things up and it would all go back to normal in a few weeks. My dad wasn't hotheaded and neither was Jimmy, as far as I'd experienced. And the options for either of them were limited. They'd most likely have to find a way to work together.

"What are you thinking about?" Charlie asked me.

"Bess," I answered, because I didn't want to say I'd

been thinking about our dads or their argument—or wondering why my dad would think Jimmy would mangle my
bike and drop it in our driveway like a warning. It wasn't a
lie anyway. I found I was almost always thinking about Bess
these days.

"Bess, yeah," he said. "I've been thinking too. About
Karen."

I turned to him. "What about Karen?"

"She's kind of the missing link. My dad doesn't
remember much about finding Bess's clothes except that
it was upsetting. And he thinks Paul's a harmless old fool.
He told me he's what we kids would call 'old school.'"

"Ouch." I cringed at the thought of Jimmy saying that.
I could hear it perfectly. Each time Charlie had broached
the subject of Bess's death, his dad had laughed him off
good-naturedly, as though he understood Charlie's journalistic impulses, was even proud of his son, but had
nothing to contribute to the story.

"Karen left," Charlie went on. "She never did interviews. She's the one person who probably knows the most
about Bess and Grant. She's not going to be worried about
talking and what people on the island will think. She's—"

"Not a joiner?" I quipped, before I could think.

Charlie looked confused. "What?"

"Nothing," I said. "Just something Nancy Jurovic said."
I didn't want to hurt his feelings by saying that's how Colleen had described him. "I just meant she wasn't part of
things. She wouldn't care what people think. You're right."

"What if we called her?" said Charlie.

"And said what? 'I'm Nancy Drew and this is Frank

Hardy. We're investigating *The Secret of the Old Lighthouse* and . . .'"

"I could say I was doing a story for the *Gazette*," Charlie offered.

"She didn't want to talk to the press at the time," I said.

"So, tell her the truth. Your mom was a close friend. You just found out about what happened and you want to ask her some questions."

"So, I'm the one calling her?"

"First of all, you're a girl. It might come off as less threatening."

"Thanks a lot," I said.

"Second, it's your mom's diary. We know from what she wrote that they were close. My mom had something with Bess about my dad, even if they were good friends. Your mom used to stay over there. Karen must have known her pretty well and liked her enough to let her stay at their house."

That made sense. "Okay. I'll call. We have to find her number though."

"Already done," he said, and turned his computer screen toward me. Karen Linsky, 262A Prospect St., Gloucester, MA, followed by the number.

As I let the phone ring, I realized I was nervous. I could feel a chill between my shoulder blades, and my palms were damp, like I was taking a math test or something. Cell phone reception at the inn had never been great, Charlie said, even before the storm. We were calling from a guest room on a land line that had only recently been brought back to life. I kept worrying Cat or Jimmy or anyone working at the inn might pick up the extension while I was talking to Karen.

The woman who answered had a rough, low voice that sounded charred by years of cigarettes. She listened without comment as I babbled the explanation of who I was, who my mother was and why I was calling. I expected her to hang up on me at every moment, but she didn't. When I finished, there was a long silence.

Then she said in her harsh, raking voice, "I don't understand why you're calling me about this now. Bess has been dead more than twenty years. It's a little late to be barking up this tree, don't you think?" She said "barking" with the classic Massachusetts accent: *bah-kin*. Then, when I couldn't think of an answer she said, "How's your mother, good?"

"She's okay," I hedged. "You know, it's funny but I think she still misses Bess after all this time."

"She was a good girl," said Karen. I didn't know if she meant her daughter or my mother. "I shoulda taken her home after Grant passed, like everybody said I should."

"Home?" I asked, confused.

"Back to Gloucester. Back where we belonged. It was a mistake, but she seemed happy on the island there." *They-ya.*

"Was she close to her dad?" I asked.

She made an "eh" noise that sounded like a shrug. "Grant was a good-time boy, even when times were bad, you know what I mean?"

"I'm not sure."

"The marina. How it all went down. He tried to put on

a show of happy, happy, but then behind that, he's scrambling to keep things afloat. For a while it looked like he had a sale to this developer, but then . . . that never happened." She gave a quick, harsh laugh. Behind it I could hear a whole life of bad luck.

"Didn't the town buy his business?" I asked.

She laughed. "Right. They 'bought' it. Like, he could either get foreclosed or they could take it over. They acted like they were doing him a favor." So, no inheritance, no jealous uncle. "He knew he was in trouble. What else was he going to do?"

"To do?"

"To get out of it."

Was I understanding her right? Charlie, who was listening with me, the handset pressed between our ears, pulled away to give me a surprised look.

"Do you mean—" I wasn't sure how to put it. "Do you think he killed himself?"

"He was a sailor first. I don't care how drunk they said he was—and he wasn't that drunk; the medical examiner even said—you don't end up off your boat and tangled in your anchor." At this, Charlie mouthed, *Anchor?*

"He was alone?" I asked. She didn't answer. Maybe she nodded, forgetting she was on the phone. There was a flick and crackle as a match was struck.

"You said something about the anchor?" I prodded.

"The anchor of the boat. He got caught up in it. That's how he drowned." I could hear her inhale, then blow out the cigarette smoke.

"Were there any other anchors? I mean, did he ever get

one delivered to him or did someone ever give him one? Or Bess?"

There was silence on the line. I couldn't tell if we'd been disconnected or if she just wasn't talking. A click and a staticky scratch on the line a moment later, followed by a dial tone, answered my question. She did not want to talk about anchors. In a movie, you would have cut to her, revealing the slab-faced, threatening guy standing next to her. Maybe he would have a knife at her throat, making sure she didn't make any false moves. But I was letting my imagination run wild. She might just not have known what I was talking about. She might have had enough of talking to some nosy kid, bringing up her dead daughter.

"Wow," said Charlie.

"We didn't even really get to Bess."

"I wonder who the developer was. Same guy who likes causeways?"

"I wonder. You know what's weird? She didn't sound upset," I said, just realizing it. "That was what I was most afraid of, upsetting her."

"It happened a long time ago," said Charlie reasonably.

"Yeah," I said. "Still."

"Still," agreed Charlie. He put his hand over mine. We sat on the old-fashioned chenille bedspread. Its snowy whiteness glowed in the lowering gloom of afternoon. Everything got very quiet. Winter was coming and I could feel that even if they got the ferry running and the houses brightly painted, nothing was going back to normal, ever.

THIRTEEN

For my Katniss costume, I'd gotten a toy bow-and-arrow set at the Stone Cove Variety Store. They'd reopened by moving all their stock to one side of the large—for the island that is—warehouse space and hanging clear plastic painting tarps from the ceiling to cover the unrepaired soaked drywall and imploded timber on the side the storm had destroyed. Once I'd gotten home, I'd spray-painted the arrows silver and made a quiver out of a roll of brown felt. I wore brown pants tucked into old riding boots (thrift store), a military-looking belt and a navy wind-breaker under a longer suede coat (thrift store again). I braided my hair. While I got ready, Mom sat on my bed and watched. She hadn't read or seen *The Hunger Games*, but I told her the story. And she loved Halloween. She'd made caramel apples to hand out to the kids, as well as the requisite supply of drugstore fun sizes.

"It's a circle pin with a bird in the center?" she asked. I didn't have something to use as Katniss's mockingjay pin. It was the last piece I needed for my costume.

"It can be any bird pin. Gold, if possible." She thought a minute, her index finger to her lower lip, almost in a "shhh" gesture. For a second, I could see the little girl in her face. Then she smiled, triumphant.

"Aha!" she said, and walked to her bedroom. I followed. She took the wooden jewelry box from her dresser and set it down on the bed between us. She drew out a gold pin, shaped like an eagle. It was a proud, mean bird, clutching something in its talons.

"Would this work?" she asked.

"Totally!" I said, excited. "It's perfect. Hers is a little more Soviet looking, but that one is great."

"Well, it's nationalistic in its own way, I guess." She pinned it to the collar of my windbreaker. "You won't lose it, right? You'll be careful."

"Of course I'll be careful." Did she know about the diary? Or was she just worrying out of habit? "I'll be really careful." My eye went to a gold chain, tangled in one of the little partitioned sections of the jewelry box. She seemed to notice it at the same time and picked it up.

"Oh," she said, slightly breathless. "I haven't looked at this for a long time. She tried to straighten it. A stiff, scripty *Elizabeth* was looped in gold and held on either side by a thin gold chain.

"After she died, her mother wouldn't let me keep any of her things. She shut the house up and took the bare minimum with her. I don't even know what she did with Bess's things. Anyway, later I found this in my room, under my bed. She'd lost it in the winter sometime. I guess one time when she'd slept over. I was so mad at Karen, but then I got to keep something after all. Now I understand how scared she was." She cut herself off abruptly, as though she hadn't meant to speak these thoughts out loud.

"How scared who was?"

"Karen."

"She was scared after it happened? Or before?"

Mom hesitated, "I really didn't know Karen that well. She wouldn't have confided in someone like me. I was a kid."

"But Bess was scared too," I insisted. This was exactly what my dad didn't want me putting my mother through, I thought guiltily. But it was like a scab I couldn't stop picking at. She brought that same finger to her lip again, then looked at me hard, her normally cool, sea-glass eyes blazing.

"It's not something you need to worry about. Eliza, listen to me. I won't let anything happen to you. Ever."

I didn't know what to say. Mom kept staring.

"Was Karen nice?" I asked, just to keep her talking.

"Nice?" she said. "Not really. She was honest though. I respected her at that age, I remember."

"Did she talk about moving away before the thing with Bess?"

"I don't know. Bess always said she threatened to, especially when Bess was younger, but we weren't really close until high school. It wasn't like you and Meredith. We weren't really childhood friends. It happened later."

"Who was your childhood best friend?"

"Your dad, of course," she answered, a little too quickly. "We were neighbors. We were in the same playgroup as babies." This surprised me. I tried to picture them, toddling around a play kitchen, throwing toy food into the toy sink.

Suddenly a new thought came to me, something I hadn't realized before, which now struck me like a brick. How had it never occurred to me? *Elizabeth.* We had the same name. *Bess. Eliza, Elizabeth.* All possibility of coincidence seemed to drain away. Was I named after Bess? Was it an accident that I'd been the one to find the letter or was it somehow my fate?

"Mom, we have the same name." She nodded.

"You should have the necklace," Mom said, suddenly decisive.

"Mom, no, it's your one memory of your friend."

"You should have it," she insisted. "It's not doing me any good hidden away in here. Besides, you share her name." She smiled a weird "go figure," smile, then threw her arms around me and crushed me to her, breathing ragged breaths I could feel through both coats. I was smothered, face pressed so hard into her shoulder. At the same time, I didn't want her to let go.

CHARLIE SHOWED UP AROUND eight, as planned. I hate it in books when writers describe people or things as "impossibly cute" or "impossibly charming," but both pretty much summed up Charlie Pender that night. I'd dreaded having him pick me up at our house. I'd offered to meet at the dance, but Charlie said no. My dad was out—he'd agreed to be a chaperone; Jimmy was another, so that would make for an interesting night—but my mother was relaxed (for her)—even friendly. Charlie had brought me a little bag of Scottie dog-shaped licorice candies, a nod to Salty.

After my dad had left for the dance, I'd rechecked the shed for the anchor. When Charlie gave me a questioning look while my mom went to get him a glass of water I knew what he meant and nodded, *Yes, still there.* He drank the water quickly and we left, my mother waving from the porch, looking almost happy.

THE NIGHT WAS COOL and clear, not yet frigid the way it can get sometimes in the fall. With the island only semi-lit, the stars blazed in the sky, even more than they might on an ordinary night. People had gone out of their way to decorate with pumpkins, witches, scarecrows and ghosts. The houses that were half-destroyed seemed to have made double the effort. Walking down my street, the darkness and quiet unfurling around us like a blanket, I didn't care if we ever reached the dance. Charlie's hand was warm in mine, and the air was crisp against my skin and for a moment I felt completely right.

"So, the anchor's still there," said Charlie, breaking the silence.

"The anchor's still there," I confirmed. Just saying the words made me feel better. As long as the anchor was there, it meant my father wasn't doing something terrible, whatever that might mean, and that I could still trust him. Or at least, imagine I could.

"You make a good Katniss."

"I do?"

"Sure. Brave, quick-witted, impulsive, ruthless . . ."

"Ruthless?" I smacked his arm.

"Okay. You're right. That's not fair. Katniss isn't ruthless, exactly, in the book. And I haven't seen the movies yet. Let's just say . . . mean when she has to be—"

"Charlie, you're pushing your luck," I interrupted. I shoved the bad thoughts aside and matched his playful grin.

"Please. Call me Clark."

I brandished a spray-painted, plastic arrow. "Fine. But don't forget, I'm armed."

THE SCHOOL GYMNASIUM WAS still full of families displaced by the storm, so a local farmer (one of the few left), Randall Moss, had volunteered to host the dance in his big hay barn on Hill Road—the road leading from the school up to the Anchor Club. It would have made more sense for me to pick Charlie up at the inn, as it was much closer to the farm, but Charlie was too chivalrous for that. As it was, we had to pass the inn on our way. Charlie looked up at the grand porch as we walked by. I thought I heard him sigh.

"What?" I asked.

"Just weird to be back. I wasn't expecting to be here this long. But it sucks you in."

I nodded. I wished Charlie could love his home as I did, but at the same time, I felt the edges peeling up on the picture I had previously painted of my life here. How much of it was an illusion for my benefit, for the benefit of all the kids and families headed to this dance?

"I'm sure your parents really appreciate having you

here to help. And it's not for much longer," I said. What I wanted to say was, *don't go,* but I couldn't say that.

Charlie didn't say anything. We walked in silence until we hit the crest of the hill, the land now rolling down toward the harbor. From the road, we could see the barn, giant doors flung open, inside glowing orange like a welcoming fire. In the night it looked like a giant jack-o'-lantern.

"Wow," I said. "Beautiful."

Charlie squeezed my hand in agreement. "Ready to leave District Twelve?" he asked. We turned down the rutted driveway.

Inside, Macklemore blared from speakers that had been stacked unprofessionally among hay bales. Everyone was there, even the kids I'd never seen at a dance before. It seemed important that night for us all to be together. Parents stood in corners in pairs or alone, looking either bored or dubious. Too many chaperones, in my opinion, for less than a hundred kids.

"I bet now you really feel like you never left," I told Charlie.

"Yeah. That's for sure. Do you want some bad punch?" he asked. "Or do you want to dance?"

"Dance," I said quickly.

I looked up at the huge orange Chinese lanterns swaying from the rafters. An old Smashing Pumpkins song from the nineties had started, and couples around us were moving onto the dance floor, or really just the middle of the floor. It was an undanceable: a half dreamy but not slow song, and kids were standing, swaying to it, unsure what to do. The dance committee had done a good job with the decorations, going for abstract, filmy fabrics and sparkly spiders, lighting everything in an orange glow rather than featuring skeletons and zombies. There had been a lot of debate about whether it was appropriate to have blood, gore and death at the dance after so much real destruction had visited the island.

Some kids had gone for a hurricane theme, covering themselves with fake plastic fish and other debris like they were flotsam washed up on the beach, or opting for the understated, high-concept costume: cutoff pants ("floods"). But most came as characters from horror movies, *Carrie*, *The Shining* and *The Blair Witch Project*—Aiden Walters had turned himself into a bundle of sticks. His date, Alison Jaffe, carried a flashlight under her chin all night—and the usual assortment of classics: popular girls as sexy kitty cats, jock-y guys dressed as girls, geeks decked out in Star Wars or costumes recognizable only to serious Comic Con insiders.

"Dance it is," said Charlie, once we'd taken in our surroundings.

"Thanks for coming back to high school."

"I would never go back for anyone but you." We waited until the next song started, an upbeat, overplayed, disco-inspired track. As we danced, I watched the parents watching us. Colleen's mom was laughing, talking to the woman who sold ferry tickets. She was dressed as some kind of old-fashioned English barmaid or maybe Swiss Miss. I wasn't sure which. Nancy and Greg Jurovic, in matching red sweaters, were toasting everyone who walked by, Nancy's a no-sleeve and Greg's a cardigan.

"Twin set!" Nancy called out in response to each confused look she received.

In one corner, at a table, sat Meredith and Tim, heads close, talking intently. Meredith looked beautiful: Snow White with very white, powdered skin and lips that were— you're expecting "impossibly" here, right?—red. Tim was dressed like an explorer or someone on safari. Indiana Jones, maybe?

I smiled. I didn't know where Pete Brewer was, and I didn't really care. He was probably out behind the barn playing some drinking game with his baseball team buddies, each of them stretching out their girlfriends' borrowed sweaters and skirts beyond repair.

I winked at Meredith when we got close enough and she smiled a shy smile and tossed her hair back, happy and embarrassed. Officer Bailey—Lynn, as I saw her now, a teenager in pimples and mom jeans—was watching me. She was not in costume other than her own off-duty version, black jeans with quilted vest. The whole time we moved around the floor, I felt her eyes on me. When I looked back at her, she looked away. I wondered if this scenario felt familiar from her own high school days: on the sidelines, watching her classmates have fun, wishing she could be one of them. She was making me uncomfortable. Charlie sensed my distraction.

"What's up?" he asked.

"It's LB. She's watching us. It's . . . I don't know. Creepy."

"So let's go outside. It's nicer out there anyway."

He was right. Even with the barn doors wide open, the air inside felt humid and overheated. We headed toward the back door that opened out onto the cow and hay fields, but when we reached the door, I saw that Officer Bailey had cut across and beaten us there. She reached one hand toward my wrist, tapping me lightly with two fingers.

"Uh, Eliza?" I expected her to say students weren't allowed out behind the barn, but she didn't. "I keep meaning to get this back to you. You left it in the diner?"

To my amazement, she held out my mother's diary.

"I thought you might need it for school," she went on. I was too flabbergasted to speak. For one thing, I had run into her one place or another almost daily since that afternoon in the diner. For another, she was pretending she hadn't read the diary, which was absurd, because if she hadn't, how did she know whose it was? And, since it had Willa Montgomery, not Eliza Elliot written on it, how could she think it was mine or a book for school or anything other than a diary?

I also was sure I had not left the diary at the diner. I had it with me that day, but as soon as Charlie arrived, I'd put it back in my bag. I had never set it down on the table or the seat next to me. She had to have taken it from my bag, either while she was sitting next to me in the booth—or, more likely, when I'd forgotten my bag on the seat, before I'd gone back for it.

Why had she kept it so long? And why was she lying to me right now? I could probably answer the second question. I cringed, imagining LB reading all the mean things about her my mom had written.

"We might need it back, at some point," she added, almost as an afterthought.

"We?" I said, surprised.

"I'll let you know if we do. Anyhoo." She took a deep breath and turned away. "Enjoy the evening, you guys. Stay safe."

Stay safe? At the dance? What did that mean?

Charlie and I walked outside where the chill air was a relief. The music receded to a distant bass throb. We leaned against the split-rail fence and looked up at the moon. It was big and low in the sky, a harvest moon.

"Pretty," I said.

"That was weird, with the diary."

"No kidding." We had not been out there five minutes when Jimmy Pender strolled up. It suddenly felt as if every adult were here to chaperone just the two of us. He stood next to Charlie, looking up at the sky, rocked back on his heels, knees almost looking bent behind him.

Jimmy Pender was a tall man, very blond with stiff hair like a brush, and pinkish skin. Charlie's brothers took after him. They had the same build and coloring. Charlie was thinner, darker haired, with looser joints and creamier skin. Tonight Jimmy was dressed as Davy Crockett, wearing a raccoon hat I hoped was fake but suspected was not.

"Hey, Dad," said Charlie.

"Beautiful evening, eh, kids?" Jimmy turned to include me in his big, showman's smile. He was always on. It seemed exhausting to me. "It's all like déjà vu being here."

"Yeah," said Charlie. "I feel like I never left high school."

"Me too, son. Though in my day, I remember we liked to throw our own parties. Didn't spend much time at official school functions." Jimmy laughed. "How about getting us some punch?" he said to Charlie.

Charlie nodded okay, but flashed me a glance before he headed back inside. Jimmy and I stood together, not saying anything. To me, it seemed like he'd deliberately sent Charlie away, but he was silent.

"Great pumpkins this year," I said. That was about the best I could come up with. Every year the inn held a carving contest, and Jimmy, as impresario, always awarded the prizes and carved a masterpiece of his own. He really was pretty good at it.

"Heard you had some trouble with your bike?"

"Yeah," I said. I didn't want him to think I thought he had anything to do with that, but I didn't want to say anything about Paul. "It was stolen. Probably just as a prank," I added hastily, not wanting to say anything bad about the island. "I got it back."

"That's good." I got the feeling he was sizing me up, looking for information, but I had no idea what he wanted. "Your dad was here earlier. I asked him to run up to the inn for ice. It's so damn hot in there we ran through it faster than expected."

"Oh," I said. I hadn't even looked for my dad. So he'd gone to the inn. Did that mean he and Jimmy had patched things up? Or was Jimmy trying to show who was boss, sending him out on dumb errands? I doubted the punch even had ice in it to begin with. The thought annoyed me.

"What's your costume?"

I started to say "Katniss." He wouldn't know the books, so I'd have to explain the whole story. The necklace my mom had given me was itching my chest. I pulled it from under my T-shirt, ran my thumb along the bottom of the scripty word. It came out before I could stop myself. It was like one of those devilish elves from a dark fairy tale put the words in my mouth and they popped out of their own free will.

"Bess," I said. "I'm here as Bess." I held out the necklace, which was plenty bright and legible in the moonlight. His face went ashen, then red. His eyes narrowed and I saw a flash in them, the impulse, just for a second, to snap my neck. At the same moment, Charlie walked up, holding three plastic glasses half filled with red juice balanced in a triangle between his hands.

"Punch all around," he said, handing the first one to me.

"Thanks. What flavor is it?" I had to force the steadiness into my voice.

"Uh. I don't know. Red?" He handed the next glass to his father, who met his eyes with a calm, relaxed smile.

"Thanks so much," Jimmy said. "I'd better get back inside, check on things. You know what they say, when the cat's away . . ." I'd heard him make that joke a hundred times, usually around his Anchor Club buddies, implying he and his buddies would be doing the playing (the mice), while his Cat was away. Of course that wasn't what he meant this time.

"You kids be good, now." He was looking right at me. Then he turned abruptly and strolled back inside the barn. Charlie held up his cup, toasting me. I returned the gesture. I wanted to hug him instead. Jimmy was dangerous. But there was no way I could tell Charlie that. I rewound the conversation in my mind and this time a particular line stood out: *We liked to throw our own parties.*

What kind of parties were those? I thought.

"Charlie," I said, dumping my punch into the grass. "I think we should go to The Slip. I want to see where Bess went that night."

FOURTEEN

The Slip was the kind of place where any time of day felt like three in the morning. The crowd there wasn't the kind to bother with Halloween dress-up. But ours weren't terribly out there. Nobody even looked up when we walked in.

I had never been to a bar on the island. We all knew how strict they were, and besides, a fake ID wasn't much use on an island where everyone knew exactly who you were and how old you were. But The Slip was out of our realm somehow. Besides being on the far side of the island, it was a dark place with no music—a hideaway for serious drinking, not dancing, fun or conversation. Everyone there looked like they had regular spots, regular orders, maybe even an indefinitely open tab. If there ever were out-of-towners, they were middle-aged men on fishing trips or on an overnight from the mainland, looking to party with their buddies. You wouldn't go there on a date, and you wouldn't go there as a high school girl alone. It had been that way since my parents were teenagers.

I didn't think I would find any clues at The Slip, obviously. I just wanted to get a feel for what it would have been like for Bess, on a night where most of the island was somewhere else. I thought somehow if I were there I would be able to see through her eyes. Was she there with my dad and Jimmy? With Cat? Why had she left alone? What had happened between the four of them? There were enough reasons for any of them to be mad at her, jealous of her, but to kill her? I couldn't imagine it.

The case was stronger for it to be some outsider, a random crime. But what if she'd received an anchor? What if it was someone from the island? I thought of the flash in Jimmy's eyes when I'd showed him the necklace, that moment where I saw he wished me dead. He could control his impulses now, but what about then?

Charlie and I found a table in the back, near the jukebox and a pool table that had deep groves scratched into the felt from many nights of drunken misses. I felt a flutter of nerves as we settled in, but the bartender didn't even seem to see us.

Eventually Charlie stood up, went over to the bar, and ordered two beers. The grizzled bartender served him without batting an eyelash.

"What are we looking for?" he asked, pushing the heavy pint glass toward me. The glass was warm, like it had just come out of the dishwasher, and the beer was warm too. I sipped some foam off the top. It tasted bitter and soapy. I pushed it aside, not wanting to drink anymore.

"I don't know," I said. "I just wanted to see what she saw that night." I realized it was ridiculous as I said it. Bess's murder had happened twenty-five years ago. I didn't know her. I couldn't see through her eyes. Wearing her necklace didn't give me some psychic connection to her. Charlie didn't say anything. "It's stupid. I see that now."

He shook his head. "It's good to look at all the angles, build the picture."

"Did you learn that at the *Globe*?"

He looked sheepish. "Nah. Jay says that."

"I'm still surprised he dropped this, just let it go so easily."

"We don't know it was easy," said Charlie. "And it's a small town. I think he just gets tired of fighting the same fights." He was looking over my shoulder into the recesses of the bar, where tables even darker and more anonymous than ours lined the back wall. Suddenly his eyes widened and he looked back at me, making a face that said I should turn and look too, but not too quick.

I followed Charlie's stare. At a corner table near the bathrooms, Mr. Malloy was sitting alone, a short glass of whiskey in front of him, staring into space. He looked like he'd been there a long time.

"What's he doing here alone?" Charlie whispered.

"Let's go find out."

"Eliza. Is that a good idea? He's your teacher and you are in a bar."

"So are you," I countered.

"I'm not in his English class. I've graduated. I can do whatever I want."

"Charlie, he doesn't look like he'll remember seeing us tomorrow. And even if he does, how's it going to look if he turns me in at school? I could just as easily bust him for being catatonic, in a bar, instead of at the school dance." I jumped up before he had a chance to talk me out of it, grabbing my warm beer more as a prop than anything else. Charlie was right on my heels.

"Hi Mr. Malloy!" I said as cheerfully as if I were running into him in the cafeteria. "Mind if we join you?"

I set my beer down and pulled out a chair. Mr. Malloy looked up at us, confused, as though he wasn't sure if what he was seeing was real or some ghostly apparition. He didn't say anything, so we sat down. If he was surprised to see us in the bar, he didn't show it. We sat in silence. I wasn't sure how to begin the conversation, especially after our last one had gone so badly. He was staring at the damp rings on the table, now that I was blocking his view to whatever faraway place he'd been looking before. After a few minutes, he looked up slowly, but his eyes caught and froze before they reached mine. He had just registered Bess's necklace.

"She did see something, before she died," he said, still not looking at me or Charlie.

"She did? What?" I asked. I allowed myself a secret sigh of relief. He was clearly either too drunk to notice that his student was drinking with him or too troubled to care. Either way, I wouldn't bring it up if he didn't.

Malloy didn't answer.

"Why didn't you ever tell anyone?" Charlie asked.

"I wanted to," the old man croaked.

"But . . ." Charlie prodded, though gently. *He'll be a good reporter,* I thought. *He can read people just right.*

"But. It was a different time then. Teachers weren't allowed to . . . that is . . . one's private life did affect one's professional life. If it were now, things might be different."

"There was something you were afraid would come out about you?" I asked, confused.

Malloy laughed a bitter laugh. "Come out," he said. "Yes, exactly. Nowadays it probably wouldn't matter. Though, who knows? This island hardly moves apace with the rest of the world."

Charlie nodded. It made sense. To keep Bess's secret, whatever that was, someone had threatened Malloy with his own secret. *I took care of Malloy,* Jimmy had said. Did he mean now or twenty years ago?

Malloy turned to me. "Since you brought her up a few weeks ago, I keep thinking, did I do the wrong thing? I kept my own secret instead of telling hers."

"Her secret," I asked. "You think that was why she was killed?"

He shrugged, for the first time looking both present and worried. He glanced clumsily around to see who might be listening. There was no one sitting close enough to hear a word we were saying, but he was clearly agitated. Maybe he was sorry he'd started talking.

"If you come with me," he slurred at me in a whisper, leaning across the table. "I'll show you what I kept. You can have it. There's no reason for me to hold on to it."

Under the table, Charlie gripped my arm. I could feel him thinking this might be a bad idea.

"Okay," I said quickly, standing before Malloy could change his mind or Charlie could try to change mine.

"If you don't mind, I'll come along too," Charlie said, standing with us. Malloy shrugged: *suit yourself.*

We left the bar, an odd threesome, me and Charlie in costume and Malloy weaving as he led us down the walkway from the bar. I hoped he wasn't going to try to drive us anywhere.

"My apartment is nearby," he said. "It's close to Bess's house, actually." It felt strange, and possibly like a bad idea, to go home with our drunk teacher. But, I reasoned, there were two of us. What could Malloy do? And it wasn't even late yet, as if bad things could only happen after midnight. Charlie walked next to me, saying nothing. I wondered if he was also thinking going to Malloy's might be a mistake. It hadn't occurred to me to suspect Malloy of killing Bess, but now I considered the fact that he'd kept something of Bess's all these years, the strange way he'd talked to me about her at school, in a trance, remembering one instant, offended that I'd mentioned her the next. But that was crazy. Malloy was a respected teacher at school. If I kept on like this, eventually I'd suspect everyone on Stone Cove of Bess's murder.

When we reached a small, low, shingled condo building, Malloy swayed to a stop.

"It's here," he said, weaving unsteadily, bouncing off the beach plum hedge as he walked up the path.

Charlie turned to me. *You sure?*

I nodded.

Inside, Malloy flicked on a lamp, the cheap metal kind that comes on a bendy arm so you can position it. The room had very little furniture, all of which was simple: catalogue stuff or items from the village thrift store. The place was crammed with books. They covered every surface, stacked in chaotic towers around the room. Malloy seemed to devour them, not discriminating against any topic. Home decorating books were stacked with Restoration comedies, volumes and volumes of Dickens, pink-and-yellow-covered ACT UP manifestos from the '80s, Greek plays, sudoku workbooks, New England histories and anthologies of poetry, unauthorized biographies of the British royal family and of androgynous '70s rock stars.

Malloy collapsed into a faded, corduroy armchair and nodded for us to sit down too. There were no other seats. Charlie kneeled on the floor while I perched on the edge of a small, creaky table, trying not to put much weight on it. Now that he was in his own home, he seemed to sober up a little.

"You're wearing her necklace," he said, focusing on me for the first time since we'd left the bar.

"My mother had it. She gave it to me." Malloy nodded, as though this made sense to him. Charlie, still wary and uncomfortable, tried to move things along.

"You said you kept something that belonged to Bess?"

"That's right!" said Malloy, springing up from the chair as though he'd just remembered something important. He walked to a large bookcase that had been built and then added on to until it filled an entire wall. He opened the lower cabinet, dug around for only a moment and emerged with a faded manila envelope that he handed to me. What appeared to be mayhem to us was obviously as ordered as the Library of Congress to Malloy.

I opened the envelope. Inside were a series of short school papers, some typed, others handwritten, all with the name Bess Linsky in the upper right-hand corner. There was an essay on Hawthorne, one on French existentialism, Shakespeare and Tennessee Williams. Malloy had not, I noticed, changed his syllabus much over the years.

"This was what you saved? Her papers from school?"

I must have sounded disappointed, because he snapped at me bitterly, "What were you expecting? Her anchor?"

Charlie and I were both struck silent.

Malloy pressed his lips together, as though wishing to trap the words back inside, but they had already escaped. "I saved her papers, yes," he said. "She was a good student. Not an exceptional student, but a very good one. I never go through my last term's work until the following. After she drowned, I still had all my class's work from the spring, so I kept hers. I thought there might be something there. Or that the police would want to see it. It was mostly superstition, though. I couldn't throw away her thoughts, her voice. It seemed like the last thing that remained of that poor girl."

The way he spoke reminded me of my mom, how she'd held on to Bess's necklace once she'd found it, and somehow that had made her feel better.

Charlie took the papers from me and looked through them, one by one. "But if these are for school," he asked, "how are they a secret?"

"They aren't," said Malloy. "What she told me is the secret. I don't even know if it's true, but it still felt like too big a risk at the time."

We waited for him to decide to continue.

He looked away as he spoke. "She came to me during the summer. She was afraid, and maybe I was the closest person, the closest adult she felt she could talk to. I found her walking home from the lighthouse one afternoon. It must have been July. She looked . . . *stricken* is the word. Under the lighthouse, she said, was a secret room. A boy had taken her there, thinking she would be impressed. She was horrified."

"What was it?" asked Charlie.

"You asked about the anchor." Malloy turned to him and then jerked his head at me. "That's where they meet, the members of the Black Anchor Society. This boy had just joined. He was impressed with himself and wanted to impress her too."

"What's the Black Anchor Society? Not the Anchor Club?" I asked. "I've never heard of it."

"No one who isn't in it has heard of it," said Malloy. "They run the island. They're behind things. Bess said there were members dating back two hundred years. When someone tries to go against them, they make sure that person gets out of the way. You get the anchor and you either shut up, leave, or—"

"Worse?" I interrupted. I couldn't help it. Charlie shot me a look.

Malloy barked a sharp rasp of a laugh. "You didn't hear that here, my dear."

"Did you go look for the room?" asked Charlie. "After she told you about it?"

"I looked. Not until after Bess. But then I looked and I couldn't find it."

"So how do you know it really exists?" I asked.

"Because someone killed her to make sure no one found out it existed." I looked at him, suddenly afraid for him. He'd kept the secret for such a long time, and now he'd told us. What would happen to him if anyone found out?

"Can I take these and read them?" I asked, holding up the envelope filled with Bess's papers. "I'll bring them back after."

Malloy nodded.

I pulled Charlie to his feet and we said good night, first asking Malloy if he needed anything. He said no. He looked exhausted now, as if he'd just survived the hurricane again. I wondered if he'd even remember any of this come tomorrow morning. Part of me prayed he wouldn't.

Outside, the temperature had dropped. I buttoned my Katniss suede coat and set off down the path at a run. Charlie jogged after me, rushing to catch up.

"Eliza! Where are you going?"

"To the lighthouse," I yelled behind me into the wind.

FIFTEEN

"Will you stop a sec?" Charlie called. "I feel like I've been chasing you all over the island tonight."

I stopped only when I reached the lighthouse. I stared up at its black silhouette, looming against the night sky.

"Don't you want to see it?"

"The room? Yeah, but is it a good idea to go in the middle of the night?"

"It's a better idea than to go in the middle of the day. Especially when we don't know who the members are, but we do know where half the island is tonight."

He considered this. "We don't even have a flashlight."

"I do." I pulled a small LED light from my quiver.

"Nice work, Katniss."

"I need to be prepared for the arena," I joked lamely. I caught Charlie's uncertain eyes. "Look, if we get caught, we can always say we were going for a romantic walk on the beach."

At that, he smiled shyly and nodded.

I'd been all over the lighthouse on the cleanup day. I could picture the ground floor in detail, and how to go up, but not how to get underneath. The ground floor was a circular concrete slab, with one door and no windows. From there, a spiral stair climbed one side of the room. About twenty feet up, tall, skinny windows started to pierce the walls at regular intervals. Higher up was the lighthouse keeper's office, where I'd found the letter—and above that the massive light itself.

"I wonder who it was," I mused. "The boy who brought her here."

The door wasn't locked. Holding my little flashlight, Charlie and I walked the inside perimeter of the ground floor, hugging the concrete wall. We found no hinged library door, no statue with a secret lever.

"What do you think?" I asked Charlie, stumped. He looked around.

"If there's a hidden door, it's not going to be in a slab of concrete."

"That's all there is though," I complained.

"There's the spiral stair." He walked over to it.

"Going up, not down."

Charlie pulled the lowest step toward him. Then he pushed it away. Nothing happened. He tried pressing and pulling on the support at the center of the stair.

"Is there a lever or something?" He shook his head. I walked over to join him. It was ridiculous. The stair wasn't going anywhere. It was as old as the lighthouse, corroded in place, hiding no secrets. I walked around behind it and looked down, realizing that the metal base of the stair was black, freshly painted, not rusted by a hundred years of salt air like the rest of the staircase.

"Charlie," I said, motioning for him to come around to my side and pointing down at the metal plate. He understood right away. Together we kneeled. I held the flashlight in one hand as we felt, half blindly, for a pull, a hook or a hinge. At last Charlie managed to wedge a couple of fingers under the edge and the whole thing tilted right up. It wasn't even that hard.

"Wow," I said.

Underneath, the spiral stair continued down into darkness. I was less proud of my Katniss flashlight now. It was next to useless. Charlie was down the steps like a flash, light or no light. I had no choice but to follow. The stairs were a narrow continuation of the ones above. I couldn't see where I was putting my feet so I pictured the steps I'd taken many times on the way up and tried to make my steps down the same size.

Charlie had made it to the bottom now and was feeling for a light. I ran my dim, mini-flashlight over the walls, trying to help out. He seemed to have found something because all of the sudden, the room was cast in dim, amber light.

"Okay," said Charlie, looking around in disbelief. We were in some kind of underground cave, the walls thick stone, the ceiling heavy wood beams. There was a long wooden table that took up almost the width of the room. Two iron chandeliers hung down above it. These were the lights we'd turned on. There was nothing else in the room.

"I feel like I'm in an Edgar Allan Poe story," Charlie said. There was no humor in his voice. He meant it.

I nodded, determined not to get freaked out when we'd made it this far. "Let's see what we can find," I said, my tone businesslike. In my head, I counted the chairs. Twenty. That must mean that there were twenty members, assuming they all attended every meeting. But maybe there were more, and not everyone showed up every time.

Slowly we circled the room, looking for something that could tell us more. I took a deep breath, aware of the stale air, the closeness of the room. Could these lights be seen from outside? There didn't seem to be any windows, but the idea gave me an uncomfortable feeling. That metal trapdoor, if it shut behind us, would we be able to push it open again? Probably, unless someone put something on top of it.

"I don't think we should stay down here too long," I said, suddenly jittery.

"I know," said Charlie. "But it may not be so easy to come back. Let's see what we can find. We'll be quick."

I made another circle of the room, then held my hands up in defeat. Charlie was crouched at one end of the table, examining the underside.

"Anything down there?" I asked. We were talking in whispers.

"No," he said. "But look. There's a seam across the middle." There was, running across the short side. "Eliza, get on the other end and pull." We each took an end and pulled, but the table wouldn't budge.

"Is there anything along the underside on your side? I feel something over here. It feels like a tab that pulls out."

I felt along my side and found the same. *How dumb*, I

thought. *Dad makes tables like this all the time that come apart so you can add leaves.* Why didn't I think of that?

"So, hold that, and let's both pull." This time, the table slid apart easily, revealing a lower surface. Laid in four even rows under glass were black and white photographs. They were lit formally, like portraits, but they were of men's hands instead of faces. In each picture, one hand was crossed over the other. The hands were all the hands of young men, but the pictures were obviously taken at different times. Some seemed new. Others looked like they could be fifty years old. We stared at them.

"Do you think those are all victims?" asked Charlie in a horrified voice.

"Nope."

"Why not?"

I pointed at one of the pictures. "Because these are my father's hands." I showed Charlie the crescent-shaped cut across my dad's left hand—that place where a hammer had made its mark, just missing his head. Here in the photograph, the injury was still new, darker than the skin around it instead of whiter, as his scar appeared now. "These are the members."

"Anyone look familiar to you?" I asked.

Charlie shook his head. I knew he was looking for his dad. "But it's hard to tell from these pictures."

"I think that's the idea." I leaned across the middle of the table to get a closer look and the surface moved under me. "Look, Charlie. There's another layer." We pushed, and the layer with the photos rolled to the side. Underneath was a deep wooden box. In it was a large, black anchor, about the size of Salty, too big to pick up or move. I reached inside to touch it, then pulled my hand back.

"Charlie!" I shrieked. "Oh my God."

The box was about half filled with short locks of hair. I felt sick. Charlie put his hands on my shoulders to steady me as he looked in.

"Okay, calm down. Take some deep breaths. We know practically everyone on the island. They aren't serial killers. They aren't in a cult."

"How can you be sure?" I whispered. My voice sounded like a stranger's in my ears. I felt sick.

"I'm sure. Maybe this is part of their initiation."

"What about Bess? Her hair was cut off."

"Her hair was found with her clothes."

"All of it?" I pressed.

Charlie didn't answer. He couldn't. After a minute, he said we should close the table up and get out of there. He was trying to appear unfazed, but I could see his hands were trembling.

"I don't want to go home," I said. "I don't want to see my dad."

"That's fine. We won't go home. We can see if the diner's still open. If it's not, we'll go to the Little Kids' Park."

We turned the lights off, first making sure we hadn't left any signs that we'd been there. I fought off wave after wave of nausea as I focused on making it back up the steps through the dark. Suddenly I didn't want to know more, didn't want to find out what happened to Bess, didn't want to find out how my parents might have been involved.

I sleepwalked the two miles back to town. In my hand

I clutched the envelope with Bess's school essays. Charlie didn't say much either. I knew he was wondering what to think as well, picturing his dad down in that room. Would I have recognized my dad's much younger hands without the scar? I thought so, but I really didn't know. Had he really not seen them, or just not wanted to?

The diner was closed. That was not really a surprise. Businesses closed early off-season, sometimes depending on the whim of the owners or the number of customers rather than the official hours. We kept walking uphill to the Little Kids' Park. I had no idea how late it was, but we didn't see anyone along the way. When we got there, we each took a swing and rocked back and forth, looking out at the streetlights, now finally illuminated once more. There were still puddles of water under the swings left from the flooding. You had to reach your toes way over to the side to push off the ground.

"Charlie," I said. "This whole time, I've felt like we were on a ride, our own secret mission, getting closer and finding out all this stuff no one else had been able to. And now I want to get off. I feel like it was a mistake to dig this up. It's not like we can help Bess now. I don't know what I was thinking."

Charlie kept swinging, nodding gently. He didn't answer.

"You think we should keep going?"

"I don't know," he said, but he said it in a tired way, like he didn't have the will to keep going on either.

"At the school, Malloy said I was obsessed with Bess because I was avoiding reality, not wanting to think about the storm and the bad things that were happening. I guess that makes sense." All I could see in my mind's eye now was that picture of my dad's hands. I pulled out some of Bess's papers, just for something—anything— else to focus on.

The first was an essay entitled "Nursery Rhymes in Charles Dickens's *Hard Times.*" The next was a reimagining of Hamlet's Ophelia as a high school girl in 1988. The last was on Albert Camus, the sweeping and grand title of which was "Camus and the Birth of Existentialism." I paged through them. Bess's writing style was at once flowery and dull. Even I could tell she wasn't a great student. I doubted Mr. Malloy would have kept them under different circumstances. It seemed to be superstition, not admiration, that had motivated him.

I started the Camus essay. He was a writer who was no longer included in Malloy's syllabus, so all I knew about him was that he was French and that there was an old Cure song about one of his books. Bess seemed to wildly admire Camus's ideas and wrote about him as though giving a rave review to an exciting movie. Most of the essay consisted of her quoting brilliant observations Camus had made about life.

I didn't have to read past the first page, because there it was: *Do not await the last judgment. It takes place every day. To breathe is to judge.* It was that weird phrase from the letter, the one that had stuck out for not sounding like the writer of the rest of the note. Now I realized that was because the murderer hadn't written it. Camus had. I didn't need to check my notebook. I knew every word of the letter by now. I handed the stack to Charlie, the existentialism paper on top.

"Look. Charlie. Look at this. And there's a whole essay on nursery rhymes. Bess's murderer didn't write the letter. Bess wrote it herself."

SIXTEEN

Charlie dropped me off at home and I went inside as quietly as I could. Salty sniffed at my ankles and gave me a questioning look, like he wondered what I'd been up to, but he didn't bark or make any noise. I got into bed but of course, could not sleep. In the morning, I was up before my parents, making coffee and even whipping up some pancake batter from a mix.

I tried to unswirl the thoughts in my head, but it was impossible. We'd spent an hour together picking apart what the letter could possibly mean, now that we knew Bess had written it herself. On the one hand, there had been no murder. I was sure Bess had faked the blood on her shirt. She had wanted to frame the Black Anchor Society members, or scare them. So there could be closure: Mom could stop feeling responsible for Bess's death. On the other hand, the Black Anchor Society was real, and my father was a member. What other crimes had they committed? Did they lure Grant out to sea the day he'd drowned? Were they involved in the developer's death?

Right now there was an anchor in the drawer of Dad's shed. What was he going to do with it?

I nearly jumped when my parents wandered in. My dad was in sweatpants and a flannel shirt, ready for whatever weekend woodworking project he had planned. My mother was still in her shell-colored, quilted robe and fuzzy slippers. She smiled when she saw I was cooking.

"Pancakes! Eliza, how nice." I smiled back. We would sit down, have a normal breakfast together and then I would figure out what to do. But before I could open the syrup, we heard the crunch of gravel on the driveway and the short wail of a police car siren. I was first at the front door, wired on adrenaline from the previous night and lack of sleep. My parents were slower to react. They stood and looked at each other, confused.

Outside, Lynn Bailey was in the drive, driving her cruiser and dressed in her sheriff's uniform. She was making a point. She was here on official business.

I waved hello, suddenly aware that I probably still had Katniss makeup smudged under my eyes. I hadn't had the energy to wash my face the night before. "Are you looking for my parents?"

She hesitated. "Mind if I come in?" It seemed like a trick question, though I couldn't really figure out what the trick was.

"Sure."

She followed me inside.

"Hi, Lynn," called my dad, spotting her from the hall. "Get you some coffee?"

"No thanks, Nate. I need to see Willa." Dad looked

surprised but stepped back to let her in to the kitchen. Mom was standing by the sink, already pouring a mug of coffee to offer her guest.

"Willa," said Officer Bailey. "I'm sorry about this. I'm going to need you to come to the station with me. You're wanted for questioning in the death of Bess Linsky."

"What?" said Mom, almost dropping the mug.

"Lynn! What is this?" My dad looked furious. He moved to stand between her and Mom.

"Sorry, Nate, but it's out of my hands. The state is involved now. They'll have a detective here this afternoon."

"No!" I yelled. "What are you doing? This is crazy!"

Dad shot me a look that clearly said I was making things worse and should shut up and leave it to the adults. But what was she doing taking my mom in? There wasn't even a murder. Of course, the only people who knew that were me and Charlie. And we couldn't prove it. Suddenly it hit me: Mom's diary. Lynn Bailey had taken it, read it and something she'd found convinced her Mom was involved in Bess's death. I'd have to reread it, figure out what she was using to base her evidence on. But first I needed to get Charlie. Officer Bailey was telling my mom she could get dressed, but then she'd have to come with her right away. She didn't read Mom her rights, so I guessed that meant she wasn't arrested officially. Yet. Or maybe that was only how things went on TV.

I scrambled around my loose bed sheets, until I found my phone. Then I texted Charlie. SUPER URGENT. CAN YOU COME HERE RIGHT NOW? I ran back to the kitchen, where Officer Bailey and Dad were waiting in a silent standoff for Mom to re-emerge from the bedroom. I rushed in to head her off.

"Eliza!" warned LB.

"Oh, leave it, Lynn. She's a kid. You've scared her and she's worried about her mom. Let her have a moment."

LB nodded, not liking it. But I took my opening. Mom was dressed nicely, almost like she was going to church. When I came in, she was just putting in her second pearl earring. I went to her and grabbed her arms.

"Mom. Listen. Don't go. They're going to try to make you say you did something you didn't."

Mom turned to look at me. Her eyes looked worried, as usual, but now instead of weak they seemed gentle.

"I know, Eliza, that you want to fix it. I know that's how you are and I appreciate it so much. But this can't be fixed. It happened and there is no way to take it back."

"But Mom," I said. "You didn't do anything. It's in your head that it's your fault."

It was on the tip of my tongue to tell her Bess might not even be dead, that Bess had written the letter herself, but I knew Charlie and I would only have one chance to prove it, and right now we had almost no evidence. Especially under the circumstances, everyone—and in particular Officer Bailey—would assume I was panicking, making it up out of desperation to save my mom.

She gave me a sad, patient smile. "You're right. I didn't do anything. And that's why Bess is dead."

I couldn't decide if I wanted to punch her or hug her. And hug her not out of love, but out of pity. She'd devoted herself to playing the victim and that was all she could ever be. She was broken. She'd decided to ruin her life over something she had nothing to do with. Over something that hadn't actually happened. Mom swept me into her arms, making the decision for me. Her body felt limp. Then she walked back out to the kitchen.

I stayed in the bedroom, like a coward. I didn't want to watch her go.

TWENTY MINUTES LATER, CHARLIE was on the front porch, breathing hard and looking concerned. I kissed him for coming so quickly and tried to explain what had happened. It all came out in a confused rush. I stopped once I got to Mom's arrest.

"But now we know Bess is alive," he said, shaking his head. "It should be easy to clear her."

"We don't know she's alive. We think she is, but we can't prove it. And my mom's not doing herself any favors. She's like Joan of Arc climbing right up onto the fire. She thinks she deserves this, even though she's not guilty. The state police are getting involved. LB said they're bringing a detective over this afternoon."

Charlie shifted from one foot to the other, glancing back toward the town. "Hope he has a seaplane or something. There's no ferry."

"I'm sure they'll figure out something. Charlie, this is seriously bad. We have to do something."

"Let's go tell Jay what we found out last night."

I looked at him skeptically. Jay had barely pursued

investigating the story when it had happened. Would he believe our story? Would he be willing to take on the Black Anchor Society? "No. We have to find Bess ourselves."

"Eliza. We have no idea where she went and no way of getting there, even if we did."

"Come on," I said. I was already halfway down the driveway. "I have an idea."

STONE COVE ISLAND SAILING Camp was deserted. The boats were tucked away in their sheds or under tarps for the winter. The gravel parking lot was empty.

"Think Hopper will forgive me?" I asked, taking stock of the situation. Hopper ran the sailing school in the summer and coached the sailing team the rest of the year.

Charlie stood a few feet back, his smile grim. "Depends on what condition the boat's in when it comes back. If it comes back."

I shot him a look. *Not helpful.* "Charlie. There's no ferry. Almost all the bigger boats are in dry dock by now. I guess we could always just wait and ride over with the state police when they take my mom to jail in Boston."

His eyes softened as they shifted to me. "I wish we could take my dad's Bristol. It's a lot bigger, a lot sturdier. It's November, Eliza. There's a reason why everyone's taken their boat out for the year." That was true. The Rhodes 19 racing boat we were about to steal—that is, borrow— was a much dicier choice for open ocean in November than Jimmy's 32-foot keelboat. We would have to watch the weather every second. But I was pretty sure we could make it as long as we were careful and didn't run into any major surprises. Anyway, Jimmy's boat would be hard to sail with only two people and I was much more willing to risk Hopper's wrath than Charlie's father's.

I spun the dial on the lock of my sailing locker and took out my foul-weather gear. Charlie had brought his from home. We also had cell phones, a radio, water, navigational charts for the bay between Stone Cove and Gloucester, emergency flares, peanut butter and jelly sandwiches, my mom's diary, and a change of clothes. I hadn't left a note for my dad. I didn't want him to know where we were going. I figured once we got out, we could call or text someone and let them know. Maybe Jay, or even Hopper. Someone who wouldn't totally freak out. Since I was a sailing instructor in the summer, I also knew the combinations to the boat locks. Racing boats are designed to be identical and without individual quirks, to keep things fair, but I still had my favorite lucky boat, *Tigerlily*. We weren't supposed to give the boats names either, but where was the fun in that?

Charlie helped me roll *Tigerlily* down to the launch. We didn't need the winch. We could roll her right in. Usually I liked to have three people to step the mast, but two would do in a pinch, especially since Charlie knew what he was doing. I felt a little guilty doing all this behind Hopper's back, but this was an emergency. I just hoped he would understand. The wind was whipping up a little, coming out of the northeast, making the wind indicator and metal sheeting on the sheds whistle and clatter. I saw Charlie look up, estimating its direction and strength.

"Fourteen knots?"

I nodded. "Maybe fifteen. I don't see any whitecaps though." That was a good sign. The boat could handle a solid breeze as long at the water didn't get too choppy. We didn't have the weight to cut through big waves, especially without a third crew. "We can reef the sail. I think we'll be fine. And a northeast wind should speed the trip. Even if it's likely to be shifty." The mainland was nine miles away. It was going to take us about three hours.

Half an hour into the trip, I could tell I hadn't dressed warmly enough. The water was frigid and the wind kicked up waves over the stern and onto my legs. With the wind pushing from behind us, we were mostly able to run, which meant the boat was fairly level in the water, we didn't have to change course much and we were moving fast. There's always the moment where you lose sight of shore in all directions. It had always given me a shiver of both fear and elation.

I looked at Charlie, who every few seconds was turning back to check the clouds gathering behind us. They were far enough away that I didn't think they were a serious threat, but the wind was strong and carrying them in our direction. It was possible they'd catch us before we reached Gloucester Harbor.

"What do you think?" I asked him.

"Looks okay," he said, a little uncertainty in his voice.

My teeth were chattering and my back and ribs ached from bracing against the cold. The icy couple of inches of water in the boat had soaked my shoes. I wished for coffee and dry boots and suddenly wondered if this whole plan was half-baked.

FOR TWO HOURS WE sailed like that, keeping the wind behind us, watching the storm clouds gain on us. My feet eventually went numb. I sat, holding the tiller and looking back over my shoulder. *Tigerlily* strained against the wind, which was a little too strong for her and the waves, which were a little too big, kept slopping more water into the cockpit. I kept one eye on the level of water in the boat. It was still a couple of inches. Nothing dangerous, but not exactly reassuring. We couldn't afford to take on much more. The scuppers, which normally drained the boat, seemed to be clogged. Because we were so cold and because we had to sit still and keep the boat level, Charlie and I didn't say much. When, a few minutes out, we'd needed to reef the sail—shorten it so it wouldn't catch too much wind and overpower the boat—we'd traded off tying down the sails and steering without a lot of negotiation.

By the time I spotted land, I couldn't feel my hands, either. I let out a little "whoop!" of triumph, and Charlie tried to match my excitement with a smile. But he looked miserable, hands and lips chapped, his eyes tearing from the cold.

I relaxed my frozen fingers a little on the tiller.

Bad move. The wind shifted to blow us from the side, hard. The sail whipped across the boat in a ragged jibe, flinging the boom and almost sending me into the water. I caught the line to the jib sail and kept myself aboard, but now no one was sailing the boat.

Tigerlily leaned dangerously and water poured in over

the side. Thinking fast, Charlie uncleated the mainsail so the wind could spill out of it, releasing its hold on the boat, and grabbed the tiller, setting us back on the right course.

My legs were soaked despite my foul-weather gear, and there was about a foot and a half of water in the boat. We were still several hundred yards from shore.

"Bail!" called Charlie, grabbing a bucket. "I'll sail the boat. Let's get some of this water out."

I grabbed a blue plastic bucket and started heaving water over the side, and kept it up for the next fifteen minutes as we limped into Gloucester Harbor.

SEVENTEEN

We found an empty slip in the visitors' dock. I was starving and wet and exhausted and freezing. The peanut butter sandwiches had ended up underwater. Originally our plan had been to find Karen Linsky's house and go straight there, but now we were too wet, too cold and too bedraggled to show up on a stranger's doorstep.

"My friend David has an apartment in town. Do you remember him? David Algado?"

I shook my head.

"He's a couple of years older. Goes to Gloucester Community College. We can change there. He'd probably even let us stay over."

I hadn't thought about the possibility that we might need more than a day to find Karen, find Bess, and make it back to the island. But now that I did, it was obviously going to take longer than just the afternoon. We didn't even have a way back to the island figured out. If the wind stayed out of the northeast, we were not going to make it back on *Tigerlily*, sailing into the wind. The idea of spending the night with Charlie, and at Charlie's older friend's place kind of made me nervous. But I went with it. My dad was going to kill me when we got back.

"Okay. Let's do that."

DAVID WAS FINISHING UP at work at a fish and chips shack near the marina, so we had to go there first. I lingered near the entrance, my stomach rumbling in the heavy aroma of grease and fried food. David seemed almost to be expecting Charlie. I wondered if he'd planned ahead for this without telling me. They exchanged a quick, hushed conversation.

I recognized David vaguely, but with his beard and scruffy hair and flannel shirt, he looked pretty much like every other college kid who partied on Stone Cove Island during the summers. He took off his apron and walked us to his apartment, without asking any questions.

The building was an ugly Victorian, four stories and painted a mustard yellow, with pinky-orange trim. Inside, it was messy—empty beer bottles and pizza boxes—but not dirty. He had two roommates, neither of whom was there. All the furniture was beige or brown, hand-me-down or thrift store sourced. So this was college life. In spite of the squalor, it had a cozy appeal. I wondered what my own dorm room would look like.

David gave us towels and I got out my one set of clean clothes—again, not thinking ahead—and took what felt like the greatest shower I'd ever had. After Charlie did the same, we went back to the restaurant, ordered fish and chips and asked David to show us where Prospect Street was. Now that I was warm, dry and drinking coffee, the last thing I wanted was to go back out into the cold wind. But we'd already eaten up so much of the day.

Prospect Street was a short walk from the restaurant. I'd always thought of Gloucester as big, almost a city, but everything was centered around the harbor. It was still a real working port, rough and busy, not worried about pleasing tourists.

Karen's street was wide and treeless, with low, squat houses painted grey or white and waist-high hurricane fencing out front. Together we walked up the concrete path to the front door. I was nervous and wanted to take Charlie's hand but that seemed, I don't know, unprofessional. The doorbell made a loud, aggressive buzz and then the door was opened by a woman who looked about my grandmother's age, with dry, brittle hair dyed brown, wearing a pink-and-grey tracksuit.

"C'n I help yous?" she asked, looking at us without any curiosity or interest.

"Um," I fumbled. "We're looking for Karen Linsky?"

"Yeah." This answer seemed to neither confirm nor deny. She stood there, waiting.

"I'm Eliza Elliot. We spoke on the phone. About Bess. Something else came up, that is—we found something and—" I was not going to explain it out here on the sidewalk. "And we were hoping we could talk some more."

"We might have some new information about Bess," Charlie added.

I half expected her to slam the door in our faces, but to my surprise, she opened it farther and nodded for us

to come into the dark hallway. We followed her back to
a small kitchen that was surprisingly bright. Obviously all
the light in this house came in through the back. It took
my eyes a second to adjust. Karen poured hot water into
an already in-use mug of tea and sat at the chipped lino-
leum table. She didn't offer us tea or ask us to sit.

I stood there staring at the surface of the table, with its
pearlescent swirls and plastic gold flecks. Finally we sat.
Karen didn't say anything.

"So," I began. "Sorry we didn't get to finish our conversation last time." Of course, she had hung up on me, but
now it seemed best to pretend it had been either my fault
or by mutual agreement.

Karen nodded.

"We're here because we think we might have some good
news for you," Charlie added. This was tricky, because if
for some reason we were wrong about Bess, we were about
to do a terrible thing to this woman. "We think it's possible
that Bess is still alive."

Karen looked up from her tea with a start. "What do
you mean, she's alive?"

"There was a letter that was found recently—actually,
I was the one who found it—a letter Bess got from the
person who killed her. Did Bess show it to you at the time?"

Karen shrugged.

"Anyway, after that we came across some essays and
things Bess wrote in school. Some of the lines in her
writing were the same as in the letter."

"How does that prove she's alive?" Karen looked suspi-
cious now. Her eyes went beady.

"If she wrote the letter herself, she might have set up the whole thing. To look like she was murdered," said Charlie. It did sound slightly absurd, now that I heard someone else say it out loud.

"Why in the world would she do that?" Karen snapped.

"We don't know," I said. I waited for her to say something. She was thinking, running the possibility through her head.

"She didn't kill herself," said Karen as though we'd just insulted her or Bess.

"We don't think that," said Charlie quickly. "That's not what we mean at all." Karen took a sip of tea.

"I appreciate you kids taking an interest," she said. "It'd be great if what you said was true. It really would. But it's too late for Bess. You can't bring her back. I accepted that a long time ago." She put her mug down firmly on the table and looked directly at me. It seemed like our invitation to go. To buy more time, I asked to use the bathroom.

"Down the hall, on the right," she said, waving one hand vaguely in that direction. Once I was back in the dark hallway, I took a gamble that I wouldn't be visible from the kitchen and went instead into the room on the left, Karen's bedroom. The room was neat, with a satiny bedspread in that same pink-grey she was wearing. She must really love that color. From the other room, I heard Charlie's voice, keeping Karen's attention engaged. I figured I had a few minutes to look around.

There was a dresser with an old-fashioned brush, comb and mirror set on it—very *Little House on the Prairie*—and on the wall above the bed, one framed poster from a museum show of Monet's sunflowers. On the bedside table were a couple of recent copies of *Us* and *People* magazines and a thick stack of newsletters, neatly stacked. As I moved closer, I saw they were from the Salem Public Library, going back about three years. I opened the top one and saw a letter from the head librarian gushing about all the exciting Halloween activities planned for October at the library. I wanted to open some drawers, but that seemed like taking it too far. Instead I just stood there, taking in the silence of Karen's tidy, lonely life.

"You get lost, hon? It's not that big a place." Karen's rough voice from the kitchen brought me back to myself.

"Oh, yeah. Thanks. I'm coming." Karen and Charlie met me in the hall—thankfully after I was out of Karen's bedroom—and she walked us to the door.

"It really is sweet," she said. "I appreciate your concern about Bess. I really do. But I learned to let it go years ago. There's no reason for young kids like you to get all caught up in an awful story like that. It happened, and now it's over."

She didn't ask to see the letter, or if she could keep Bess's essays.

CHARLIE AND I WALKED back down to the wharf and found a diner where we could talk, safe from the cold.

"Plan B?" Charlie asked as the waitress placed two mugs on our table. I had switched from coffee to hot chocolate with whipped cream. "She's not going to help us find Bess. She didn't believe anything we told her."

"I don't know about that," I said.

"What do you mean? I expected her to jump all over any possibility Bess was alive. It doesn't make sense."

"Unless she already knows Bess is alive," I said. "I went in her room. She had no pictures of Bess. No stuffed animals or trophies from school. Nothing with Bess's name on it. You could imagine her being too upset to have any reminders of Bess around, but she wasn't too upset to talk to us. She seemed surprised when we told her we thought Bess was alive, but not upset. Or hopeful."

"So?" Charlie asked.

"So, maybe if she knows Bess is alive, maybe if she is still in touch with Bess, she doesn't need pictures and trinkets to remind her of her dead daughter. She doesn't need any kind of reminder."

"What was in her room?"

"Not much. A museum poster. A stack of library newsletters. Nothing that helpful."

"So how are we going to find Bess?" asked Charlie.

"I don't know. I guess we'll have to try to think like Bess would."

EIGHTEEN

Back at David's, I texted Dad to tell him I was with Charlie and that I was too freaked out to come home. Charlie texted Jay, too—with the truth, just so that one person back home would know where we were.

I reread all of Bess's papers and Mom's diary, but nothing jumped out. David's roommates were both home now and though they were nice guys, the apartment was small and I felt in the way. They sat on the couch watching a Patriots game while Charlie and I spread out our papers on the kitchen island and hunched over them, combing for clues.

"We should have asked Karen about their relatives. We don't know anything about her family. She could have moved away to someplace a cousin or an uncle lives."

"We could go back tomorrow and ask her," I offered.

Charlie looked doubtful. "I think she's pretty much done with us."

"I wish I'd asked my mom," I said. Charlie didn't say it out loud, but I knew we were both thinking: *too late now.* "There's just . . . She could have gone anyplace." He nodded.

I wandered the kitchen, pacing a little. Sometimes I find moving around makes my brain work better. David had a funny collection of coffee mugs on a shelf above the sink: lobsters with giant claws, a mug with jokes about Boston, a crossword puzzle mug, a lacrosse mug, and even the famous Stone Cove Island rose cottage mug. I felt a pang of guilt that I hadn't even told Meredith where we were going, but I hadn't wanted to get her in trouble for knowing and not telling anyone, especially with the police involved.

Above the collection of mugs was a big map of Gloucester and Salem Sound tacked into the wall. I located Karen's house on it, and David's place, the street with the diner where we'd had hot chocolate, and the visitor's dock, where I hoped *Tigerlily* was still tied up safely. On the very right edge of the map was Stone Cove Island. To the north was New Hampshire, only about an hour away, and to the south, Manchester and Salem. Between the two was an island colored in green, which meant it was a wildlife preserve or park. Great Misery Island and Little Misery Island floated side by side, just offshore from Salem. I laughed to myself about the names until I suddenly remembered.

"Charlie," I said. "Can you pass me Bess's papers? Isn't there one on *The Scarlet Letter*?"

"Yeah," he said. "Here." I knew that Hawthorne lived in and had written *The Scarlet Letter* in the town of Salem. Since Stone Cove didn't have many celebrities of its own, all schoolkids were taught about famous locals from the area, which the island claimed as its own. Alexander Graham Bell, the painter Edward Hopper and Nathaniel Hawthorne featured prominently on this list, as did *Perfect Storm* author Sebastian Junger, even though he was technically from Boston, but since the book was set in Gloucester, they counted him.

I glanced down at Bess's paper, "Pearl: Hester's Curse and Salvation in *The Scarlet Letter.*" Pearl, I remembered, was Hester Prynne's illegitimate daughter, the one who causes her village to pin the red letter *A* for adultery on Hester. We had read the book the previous spring. But that's not primarily what I was thinking about. I was thinking about how the nickname Bess had given Stone Cove was Misery Island.

"What's up?" asked Charlie, interrupting my train of thought. "You're a million miles away."

"Why is Karen going all the way to the Salem Public Library when she has a perfectly good library a block from her house? We passed it on the way from the harbor." Charlie looked uncomprehending. "Bess had a thing about Salem. She identified with the main character in *The Scarlet Letter.* She was in *The Crucible* at school, that play about the Salem witch trials. She nicknamed Stone Cove "Misery Island." It's right here on the map. A little island off the coast in Salem Sound. And her mother subscribes to the Salem Public Library newsletter, even though I didn't see a single book in her house, only magazines."

"She could get magazines at the Salem Library."

"Or at the Gloucester library, a block from her house."

"Well. It's a good place to start, for sure."

"I wish we could go there right now." We couldn't do that of course. It was ten o'clock at night. But Charlie looked up the bus routes on David's computer and found a bus that would get us to Salem the next morning. It was only forty-five minutes away. He Googled Elizabeth Linsky, looking for Salem addresses and, as expected, found nothing.

"She could be married. Even if she's not, I'm sure she would have changed her name. She's supposed to be dead, after all. And I'll bet half the women living in Salem are named Elizabeth."

"That's probably true," said Charlie. "But it's not that big a town. We'll just have to scope it out, see what we can find."

I knew he was right, but it was hard to be this close and not know for sure. I wished we had thought to bring a copy of the school yearbook with Bess's picture. That might make it easier to recognize her.

Charlie and I had bought some travel toothbrushes at the drugstore and I had a long T-shirt with me I could sleep in. David had generously offered us the sofa. He and his room-mates had cleared out of the living room, but I could still hear them in their bedrooms, playing music, talking on the phone. One was working out with hand weights and they made a muffled, rhythmic *clonk* sound every time they hit the carpeted floor. Just knowing they were on the other side of the thin walls made me uncomfortable. I had never spent a whole night with Charlie, and I'd certainly never slept in the same bed as him. Not that we were going to actually, you know, sleep together, but I still felt jitters.

I stayed in the bathroom a long time, brushing my teeth,

staring at myself in the mirror and wondering how I'd gotten here. Had I really stolen a boat, sailed across open ocean in winter weather to chase after a dead girl? The person who would do that was not a person I recognized, just as I did not recognize my father as someone who would be part of some threatening, mafia-like group. Had he actually done terrible things? Or was the Black Anchor Society more like a fraternity, something he'd gotten into because his friends were doing it, because he was a joiner? I didn't want to tell Charlie this but I suspected that if Jimmy was part of the Society too, it was likely he was running it. I couldn't imagine he wouldn't bring the same take-charge, can-do attitude he brought to every other project he took on.

I imagined Lynn Bailey striding up to our front door to arrest my mother. What had made her decide to do that? Or had someone else suggested the idea to her? I had reread Mom's diary again and again. There was nothing to implicate her that I saw. I thought of the LB my mom had written about, the lonely, outcast girl who longed to be included by the popular kids. Now she was the sheriff, officially in charge. But was that who she still was underneath? Had someone convinced her to go after my mother and she was just carrying out orders? If that were true, that had to rule out Dad, didn't it? He would never allow my mom to be taken away and charged with something she didn't do.

I stayed in the bathroom so long that finally I heard a gentle tap and Charlie's voice at the door.

"You okay?" he asked.

"Yeah. I'm good. Just trying to put everything together and I think I got lost in my head somewhere. But I'm back now." I opened the door and pulled the T-shirt down toward my knees, feeling shy. Charlie had arranged a layer of random blankets and pillows on the couch for us. It looked more like a squirrel's nest than a bed, but seemed pretty cozy and warm, which was the main thing. Charlie was wearing a white T-shirt and boxer shorts. I couldn't figure out if it felt weirder to look at him or not look at him.

I climbed onto the couch first and Charlie followed, pulling the blankets up to our chins. The air in the living room was cold, but under the slightly itchy blankets, it was warm. The heat from Charlie's skin radiated out and wrapped around me. I could feel every point where our bodies touched as though each was in close-up under a microscope: my stomach against his, his hand along the side of my thigh, the tops of my toes against one shin. Our faces were so close in the dark I felt the flutter of his eyelashes against my cheek. Charlie wrapped his free arm around my shoulders and pulled me closer, until there was no space at all between us. I looked at the gold flecks in his eyes, thinking I could count them.

"This isn't how I pictured our first night alone together."

"Me neither." I laughed. "Especially the alone part." In the next room, the free weights clanked together and hit the floor with a soft thud. Whichever roommate that was had switched to push-ups, and we could hear the creak of the floor and the sharp "heh" of each exhalation. Charlie laughed too.

"Yeah. The alone part, definitely. But I'm not complaining." He kissed me.

I didn't really sleep. I drifted, waking periodically to

think, "Oh. That's my arm wrapped around Charlie's ribs" or "Those are my feet, tangled with Charlie's feet." It was restful in its own way, a half-dream state that never went all the way to consciousness or unconsciousness. Charlie seemed to really sleep, but in the morning he seemed more tired than I felt. As soon as the hard light came through the blinds I was awake. Then I just lay there, alert, my eyes clear and wide open, as if I'd already had a few cups of coffee. I didn't feel like I would need sleep again, ever. After what seemed like about an hour Charlie woke up too. He was groggy, eyes unwilling to open, burrowing back into the warmth of the blankets.

"Hi," he said, half asleep.

"Hi," I whispered back. "We'd better get going before these guys need their living room back." Charlie nodded, eyes shut. It took another half hour or so for either of us to leave our nest on the sofa, pull on whatever clothes were dry enough to wear and slip out quietly, leaving a thank-you note for Dave.

OUTSIDE IT WAS SO relentlessly cold I could feel the air freeze the insides of my nostrils each time I took a breath. Terrible weather for walking around Salem with no idea what we were looking for. I felt slightly better after coffee and oatmeal at that same diner, but was still kicking myself for not having planned better. Had I imagined Bess would be standing on the visitor's dock, waving and ready to come aboard as we pulled into Gloucester? Of course we weren't going to find her in one afternoon. We didn't even know where to start, really. I was basing my whole theory on a school play, an eleventh-grade essay and a joke she'd made once to my mom. As we waited for the bus, I reached up and ran my thumb along the sharp underside of Bess's necklace, willing some psychic connection to take place. *Are you in Salem, Bess? Are you even alive?* Not surprisingly, I got nothing back. Next to me, Charlie hopped from foot to foot, trying to keep warm, periodically tossing me a grin that said, *This is so crazy, right?*

The bus finally arrived. I had just gotten fully warm again when it dropped us in front of the Salem Public Library, the first stop in town. Charlie turned to me and shrugged.

"May as well start here." We hopped off, the wind biting our faces as soon as the bus doors opened. The library was a beautiful three-story red brick building, with a widow's walk on the roof, two big chimneys and brown trim. The entrance was kind of grand, with four columns and gold lettering that spelled out its name. I pushed the double doors open and walked in, not pausing to come up with a strategy. Inside, the room was bright, with light blue carpeting and honey-colored wood shelves. It looked like the library had been renovated not long ago. As we stood in the lobby, Charlie's cell phone buzzed. He pulled it from his pocket and looked at it, drawing the disapproving look of the young librarian on duty.

"It's Jay," said Charlie, reading the screen. "He says he's holding off our dads. Told them we took a day trip to Boston and hit bad weather. Your mom is still on the island at least for another day. Oh, and Hopper says call when you get back."

I swallowed. I'd known that was coming, but still, I dreaded being in trouble. *Always the good girl,* I thought. And being that good girl had kept me blissfully ignorant; I posed no threat. Not until now.

"How did Jay say we got to Boston?"

"Don't know," said Charlie.

The librarian was approaching us. She was petite, dressed in somber autumn browns and her dark hair was pulled back in a tight ponytail, but she looked friendly enough. Her smile was relaxed and familiar somehow.

"I'm sorry," she began, "but we don't allow cell phones to be used in the library."

"Oh, I'm not going to talk on it," said Charlie, holding it up to show he was reading a text, but he put it in his pocket anyway.

"May I help you?" she asked.

"Uh," Charlie faltered. "We were hoping to look up ferry schedules. If you have a computer?"

"Actually," I launched in. "We are researching a biologist in the area who works with the Misery Island Wildlife Foundation." Obviously I was winging it. Was there a foundation? The librarian nodded, so I went on. "Her name is Elizabeth Linsky?" The librarian didn't react, but I saw something click behind her eyes and a distance went up between us.

"Oh," she said. "I'm not sure about that. But I'd be happy to show you the computers and our nature section. There may be some books on local ecology there that would help."

"Thanks," I said. Once she left us with the ecology books, Charlie said, "Biologist Elizabeth Linsky?"

SUZANNE MYERS

"She knows Bess. Or knows something about her. Did you see?" Charlie shook his head. "Well, stay here and look like you're researching. I'm going to see what I can find out."

I followed the stack until I got to the one closest to the librarian's desk. I stood on the far side, pretending to read a self-help book. Through the shelves of books, I could hear our librarian on the phone, talking in a hushed voice.

"I don't know, but they asked about you by name. Maybe so. They're still here. Should I have Mary bring your things? She could meet you there. She's just back from lunch." At that point, Mary, who must have been another librarian, walked up, because I heard a new voice.

"Phew! You can't belicve how cold it is out there. Is Willa back?"

"No," said the first librarian. "Actually, she's not feeling well. She went home. I was wondering, you're leaving early today, aren't you? Would you mind dropping her things by at home? She left some work here."

"Not at all. Poor Willa. There's something bad going around for sure. Change of season, I guess."

I was practically holding myself up by the bookshelf. *Willa?* What was going on here? I was sure the librarian had been talking about us, and I had assumed she was talking to Bess. I decided to try the ploy that had helped me at Karen's. Rounding the end of the self-help stacks, I put on my friendliest smile and walked right up to the young librarian.

"Hi again," I said. "Would you mind telling me where I can find a bathroom?"

"Surely," she said with a serene, professional smile. For a moment she was distracted from the pile of books and folders she was trying to scoop up off the desk. I had time to read the name on the top file, before she whisked it into a canvas public radio tote bag.

Willa Prynne.

I thanked her, turned and went off vaguely in the direction she'd pointed me, then looped around and back to Charlie, who was on the computer, working on figuring out a way back to Stone Cove Island.

"They haven't posted updated ferry schedule information, just the old schedule. And we know that's wrong."

"I got it." I grinned at him. I was proud. I couldn't help it. "And you won't believe the name she came up with."

"That's amazing! Now we can look up her address."

"We don't need to. We can just follow Mary."

CHARLIE AND I HAD zero experience tailing a person, but we didn't need to worry that Mary would notice she was being followed. She walked (Bess must live close), listening to her iPod and singing along, stopping every few yards to say hello and chat with someone. The hardest thing was how slowly she went. It really was freezing. But the cold didn't seem to bother Mary, whatever she had said inside. She must have just been making conversation, which, I now observed, was something she loved to do.

At last we turned onto a little street with brick sidewalks and pretty little clapboard cottages. They were small, but modeled after the grander versions I'd seen around town. Mary walked up the path to one, a cheerful little yellow house with window boxes filled with evergreen bows. When she knocked, the door was opened by a woman in her forties with short, straight brown hair. "Mom hair," I'd heard Colleen call it. It was something between a bob and a bowl cut. Even without the yearbook, there was no doubt it was Bess. That face was still beautiful, pixie-like despite the lines, and kind. But like my dad's face, it had lost the hope it wore in those old yearbook pictures. Her eyes were soft now, without their former spark.

I elbowed Charlie, in case he hadn't come to the same conclusion, but of course he had. Mary handed the books and files to Bess, who nodded thanks. From where we were squatting, behind a low yew hedge, it was impossible to hear exactly what she was saying. But as soon as Mary was safely back on the sidewalk, Charlie and I made a beeline for Bess's door so we'd get there before she closed it.

"Willa!" I called, to keep her from turning back inside. It was super weird hearing my mom's name come out of my mouth. Bess turned, saw us, and looked puzzled. Charlie and I kept striding toward the door.

"Yes?" she asked as we reached the threshold.

"I'm Eliza Elliot," I told her. "Willa's daughter."

Her entire body stiffened. She stood, frozen, still as a statue. For an instant, the crow's-feet around her eyes seemed to flatten. She was a frightened kid all over again.

"The real Willa, I mean."

That seemed to break the spell.

"And I'm Charlie Pender, Jimmy's son," Charlie stated.

When Bess was able to breathe again, I glimpsed her search of our faces, looking for signs of our parents hidden there. Had she kept up on island lore? I wondered. Did she know which of her old friends had married each other?

She stepped back with almost the same gesture her mother had used to let us in. Sighing, she ushered us into a warm sunroom off the kitchen and offered us coffee. A shy smile tugged at her mouth. The spark I thought had vanished forever appeared in her eyes. I glanced at Charlie, who was clearly as baffled as I was. Was it possible she wanted to get caught? She looked more like a kid than ever.

"Well," she said playfully. "How is your mother?"

"You took her name," I shot back. This was no game. I needed to know what had happened that night before we could chitchat about how much time had passed.

Bess stepped closer to me. The crow's-feet had returned. Her eyes were slits. "I took her name to honor her. I miss her. I thought of her all the time after I left. So when I came to Salem, I changed my name to Willa to remind myself. She was my best friend."

"And Prynne from *The Scarlet Letter*."

She looked away. "Yes."

"Don't people ever comment on your name?" asked Charlie.

She laughed emptily. "You would think. Once in a while at the library."

"Willa's not so great, so you know. You asked how she is. Not great. First of all, she's spent her whole life blaming herself for your murder."

Bess's jaw went slack. Her lips trembled. "What? Why?"

"Because she didn't help you. She didn't tell anyone about the letter. She didn't go to The Slip with you."

"That's ridiculous!" Bess cried. "I told her not to tell. And I told her not to come that night."

"She remembers it differently. I have her diary. You can read your whole story, if you like. But right now she's being held under suspicion of your murder."

"We need you to come back. Show everyone you're alive. Get Willa released," said Charlie.

Bess's entire body shook now. She collapsed into a seat at the kitchen table. "No. You don't understand. I can't. I can never go back there. Not even for Willa."

"Bess, your 'death' almost killed my mom. Literally. And now it's all happening again. You have been living with her name all these years. You have to help her. You're the only person who can."

Bess stared down at her feet, shaking her head in a rhythmic motion of, *no, no, no.* We heard the jingle of keys in the door.

"Mother?" a voice called as the front door swung open. It was the young librarian. When she saw us, she stopped, and we all stared at one another. *Mother,* I thought. I shouldn't have been surprised. After all she had been the one to call Bess and warn her. She met my eyes and I could see her scrambling for something to say. Then suddenly, she seemed to give up the effort and threw a half smile, arching one eyebrow. It was the "Who, me?" expression I had seen on my father's face a thousand times. Bess nodded for the girl to join us and said to me and Charlie, "This is my daughter, Natalie."

I looked at the girl, unable to respond, then a single word left my mouth in a gasp, like someone drowning.

"Pearl," I said.

NINETEEN

"Let's all sit down and talk about this," said Bess, once the four of us had recovered enough to move. It was hard to know what to do next.

"Natalie," I said. "As in Nate." There was no point pretending the elephant in the room hadn't pulled a chair right up at the table with us. Bess nodded.

"As in Nate," she said. Natalie shot me an almost embarrassed glance. I couldn't read how much she knew about all this.

"That's why you left," said Charlie at last.

"That's mostly why," said Bess.

"But why fake your death?" he asked. "There must have been a simpler way."

"I was going to tell Nate," she said. "Right until the night he took me to the lighthouse, I was planning to tell him. I didn't expect him to do anything about it. I had already decided to keep the baby, but I didn't expect Nate to marry me or drop out of school or anything. Then he took me down there and showed me where they met. He was so proud. He and Jimmy had just been initiated. I made my decision then and there. But I didn't want to get Nate in trouble." Her voice faltered for a moment.

"You loved him," I said.

She swallowed and nodded. "And once I understood that he thought it was wonderful rather than horrifying—manipulating people, threatening them, keeping out anyone who was different, getting rid of the ones that got in your way—I knew there was no point telling him. So I just decided to go. I thought the letter, plus the hair, and painting the anchor on the door would be enough to expose them without it falling on Nate. Or Jimmy."

"But no one got the reference about the hair," Charlie said. "And no one found the letter."

Bess shrugged. "There was nothing I could do about that. I couldn't go back. Partly I think Mom threw them off by painting over the door. She didn't like that part of the plan, because she didn't want people thinking our house had been targeted. It made no sense, since we weren't staying, but she was sensitive after my dad was killed. About feeling like an outsider. She painted over the anchor in the middle of the night, after I was gone. We had a big fight about it later."

Charlie and I exchanged a glance. "That's why some people said there was an anchor." I said. I turned back to Bess. "How'd you get off the island?"

"Fishing boat from Gloucester. Old friend of my dad. I won't tell you which one, so don't bother asking. It was easy. Nothing was going on in the marina that night. Everyone was at the fair or at The Slip. I kept waiting for something to come out in the news about the letter. I guess I hid it too well."

Nobody spoke.

"It's amazing it never surfaced before now," said Charlie.

"There wasn't much of an investigation," Bess said bitterly.

I found that once I started looking at Natalie, I could not take my eyes off her. I studied her, feature by feature. Was her nose like mine? Like my dad's? Anything about her eyes? Her hands? Something about the slope of her shoulder? While I did this, she kept looking at me too. She would look away, and then look back. But at least she didn't seem angry. Just curious.

I wondered if she had grown up knowing about me or had thought of herself, like I had, as an only child. I was not the kind of kid who had longed for a brother or a sister. I had never felt like my family was missing something. And if I had occasionally imagined a sister, while bored and playing alone in the woods or on the beach when I was really little, it would not have been this grown-up, fully formed *woman*. She seemed so alien to me, with her placid brown eyes, her rosebud mouth and polished nails. But then, every few minutes, I would catch the flicker of my dad across her face.

"Natalie as in Nate," I repeated out loud. There was no need for Bess to answer this time. "Does he know?"

"No," she said, sounding a tiny bit defensive. There was a long silence. Even Natalie, reserved until now, squirmed.

"Bess," I asked finally. "When my dad showed you the Society's meeting place, how did he explain it? What was he expecting to have to do as a member?"

Bess looked uncomfortable. "He didn't tell me. He

talked a lot about tradition, the island's heritage and the honor of being invited to join. I didn't know what he expected. But I knew what happened to my father."

"You knew? What did happen?" asked Charlie.

"My Uncle Paul saw him go out with Jimmy's dad and a bunch of other guys, his friends. Dad called them the 'Yankee good old boys.' They went out together, in two boats, and only one came back."

"Didn't Paul tell anyone at the time?"

Bess shrugged. "Let's just say . . . he's an unreliable narrator. And my dad was just unreliable in general."

"Did they send him a black anchor beforehand?" I asked.

"They drowned him with one," Bess said, her voice flat.

"I understand why you left and why you did it that way. But it didn't stop the Black Anchor Society. And my mom really needs your help now. Plus, my dad should probably meet Natalie, don't you think?"

"I can't go back," she said. She watched my reaction and Natalie's, gnawing at her lip until I thought she might draw blood. "I'd like to help Willa. But I can't."

KAREN KNEW THE FISHING boats in Gloucester, but she also knew the freighters, the ones Stone Cove Island used to bring food and supplies over. She reacted without much fuss to Bess's decision—concession, really—then got on the phone and made a few calls. They weren't supposed to take passengers on the cargo ships, but by 5 P.M. that evening, we found ourselves on the deck of one, the *Marie Louise*, in the dark, pulling away from Gloucester Harbor. I could see how much Bess dreaded going back, but I couldn't read Natalie. She kept the same even expression as she watched the wake roll away behind the boat.

I USED TO TOSS around the phrase "my dad will kill me" the way another kid would. But I never would anymore. Jimmy Pender might very well want to kill me—I couldn't predict what my mom or Lynn Bailey would do. I was pretty sure I was doing the right thing, but it was going to be hell. I tried to be as brave as Bess and Natalie were acting. There was going to be a lot of anger on the island, when we showed up. Even those who weren't guilty of terrible things had been tricked.

Charlie stood at the railing with me, shivering. "You okay? You want to go inside?"

I shook my head. The wind whipping through my hair made me feel focused, alert. And oddly, the smell of the sea air and gentle heaving of the boat soothed my frayed nerves. "What do you think your dad will do?" I asked him.

"He always manages to work things out so they go his way. He's going to be mad for sure, but I'm not going to stick around for much of that."

He was right, I realized. He only had about six weeks before Northwestern started, and he could always go back to Boston early if he wanted to before that.

"You won't go right away, will you?" I asked.

"Not right away," he said.

I turned to him. "Are you upset that he's in the Society?"

Charlie thought for a minute. "I'm not surprised. Even before I knew about the Society, I knew he was in something.

The night we were in the lighthouse, I didn't recognize his hands in the photos, but really, I didn't need to."

"Do you think your brothers know? Are you going to tell them?"

"I imagine they're already part of it. I'm the black sheep, remember?"

"Baa," I said. But the joke sounded halfhearted, even to me.

"Meanwhile, you have a sister."

"Yeah. I don't know what my parents are going to do with that information."

Charlie shook his head. "How could you?" he murmured, squeezing my hand. "Really adds a wrinkle, huh?"

WE THOUGHT OF GOING to Officer Bailey as soon as we arrived, but instead, we ended up going to my house first. After all, we owed it to Natalie. Her Natalie story was even bigger than the Bess story. And my father deserved to find that out first, whatever it meant for our family. We were mostly silent on the way, walking up the hill through the dark streets, until Bess spoke up.

"Part of the reason I left Willa was because I knew Nate would take care of her. I knew she'd be okay."

"He was her best friend," I said, repeating Mom's words.

Bess nodded. "The hurricane really walloped the island, didn't it? I was expecting things to be the same. It's the kind of place where everything stays the same."

"It was the same," I said. "Until about a month ago."

When we turned the corner onto our street, Bess paused. "I'm scared to see Nate," she admitted. I didn't want to ask if she was scared to introduce him to Natalie or if she was scared about how she would feel when she saw him. I didn't want to know. Natalie said nothing. She kept glancing around, squinting into the darkness, as though she'd lost something. Maybe she thought she was trapped in a dream, about to wake up. I wondered what could possibly be going through her mind.

Instead I just said, "It'll be okay."

WE FOUND MY DAD heating up soup, alone in the kitchen. I entered first. Dad had spent so much time worrying about and taking care of my mother that without her he seemed a little adrift. I tiptoed in, bracing myself for the parental storm I knew I deserved, but instead my dad gave me an exhausted smile and a big hug.

"You didn't really steal one of Hopper's boats, did you?" He sighed.

"Where'd you hear that?" I hedged.

"Eliza, it's not that big an island. Want some soup?"

I shook my head. "I thought you'd be mad."

"I am mad. But right now I'm working on keeping your mom out of jail. The truth is, you're here, you're obviously fine. I don't know what you and your boyfriend got up to with your little field trip to Boston, and I don't really want to know." He ran a hand over his stubble and sat back down. "I can't afford to lose my entire family right now."

"I think I can help with that," I said. Under my breath I added, "In a couple of ways."

"Is that so?" He was stirring the soup, not really listening to me and definitely not taking me seriously. It seemed like Bess's cue.

"Dad. I have kind of a surprise for you . . ."

She walked in, Natalie behind, her shadow. Dad stared at her. He didn't even need a double take to recognize her.

"Oh my God," he whispered.

Bess cleared her throat. "Nate. I'd like you to meet my daughter, Natalie. Our daughter."

BREAKING THE NEWS TO my mom went a little differently. I figured showing up with Bess and Natalie in tow might be too much of a shock, so I decided to tell her myself.

Dad agreed this would be the best approach. Charlie went with me for moral support. I tried hard to stay focused, preparing myself for whatever reaction she might have. But it was hard. I had so many questions of my own, like, now that Dad knew about Bess and Natalie, would he still choose us? Would he have chosen us if Bess had stayed? I tried to push the uncertainties from my mind. I had to stay calm and confident when I talked to Mom, or she would sense it and it might unravel her.

"She's alive," my mom repeated, after Charlie and I had taken her through the story step-by-step. She repeated it, over and over like a mantra until I had to jump in.

"Mom, part of the reason she left was because she was pregnant. She has a daughter now. My half sister." Half sister sounded less shocking somehow than "Dad's daughter." "The other reason she left is that Dad and Jimmy and some of their friends were involved in something bad, something that really upset her." Mom nodded.

I couldn't tell whether that was because she already knew that piece of the story or if she was acknowledging that she understood it now.

"Don't worry." It was the last thing I expected her to say. In fact, I wasn't sure I'd ever heard her say that. She pulled me to her, wrapping her thin arms high around my shoulders and resting her chin on the crown of my head. The gesture transported me back to age six, sitting with her in the window seat of our living room, a snowy day, stuck at home with strep throat.

"I've missed Bess so much," she said.

"She calls herself Willa now."

Mom laughed. It was a giggly, girl's laugh. "Well, that will certainly be confusing."

"Involved in something bad?" interrupted Lynn Bailey, who had insisted on being present for this conversation and so had listened to the whole thing. Really, I didn't care. She was going to have to hear it all anyway. But someone with more grace would have let us talk privately first. Charlie and I weren't looking to keep secrets. Quite the opposite.

When we'd had a chance to fill her in a little, especially about Bess's version of what had happened to Grant Guthy, LB's face darkened. "I'm going to ask Jimmy to come down. And Nate too." Charlie's grandfather and most of the "Yankee good old boys" were dead or very old at this point. Jimmy was the youngest in a big family and his father had been over forty by the time he'd been born. There wouldn't be much LB could do to them.

"I'd like to see Bess," said Mom. "Will she come down

as well?" She seemed past surprise, and lighter somehow. Stone Cove Island's police station was tiny, but by 10 P.M. that night, it seemed like half the island was there. Bess and Natalie arrived first, with my dad. Bess and Mom could not stop hugging and staring at each other. Mom barely looked at Natalie or Dad. That was going to take a while to untangle, I thought. Both Natalie and Dad sat apart and alone, avoiding each other's eyes.

When Jimmy and Cat arrived, they looked stricken. I'd never seen either so afraid. But of course: they each thought the other killed her. And they had lived the last two decades having been fine with that. *Poor Charlie*, I thought.

"Jimmy," Officer Bailey said before he could ask a single question, "we're going to have to sit down and have a real talk about all of this. There are some things that have come to light. Some things that need a lot closer investigation."

His jaw tightened, and his eyes flicked to Dad. But Dad just kept staring at the floor. For a second, I wondered if Jimmy was going to make a run for it. But Cat looped her arm through his, her own face a mask of resolve, as if to say: *None of you people can touch us.* But that was a lie. Too many people knew the truth now.

I took one last look around at the train wreck Charlie and I had set in motion. It was like a sweater unraveling, one stitch at a time. I thought of a song Mom liked, by an old band that was popular before I was even born . . . a jokey sort of song about destroying a sweater. The refrain dared you to pull the thread while you walked away. And that was Bess, pulling the whole island's thread when she walked away, setting in motion the events that would leave the true Stone Cove naked and exposed.

"Should I walk you back?" Charlie was asking me, bringing me back to the present. I nodded. There wasn't much more for me to do around here anyway. And I knew that Dad needed time alone with Natalie. Maybe I would too, sometime. But not now.

ON THE WAY HOME, Charlie and I each kept starting to say something, then stopping. It was hard to know where to begin. We passed the village green, where the salt-burned grass had turned its normal winter brown. Lexy's dad's candy store was almost ready to reopen. There were just two windows still boarded up, waiting to be fixed. The fallen trees were gone, making Water Street look bare. The trees and grass would grow back. The buildings would eventually be repaired and repainted, but I didn't think I would ever be able to look at the island again without seeing all its scars.

A cold, damp blanket of dense fog had settled over everything. My house looked small in it, its little porch light fighting mightily under the cloudy weight. I thought of Abby and Colleen and Meredith, of the "myth" of the black anchor. I wanted them to keep believing that it was a myth. But that was impossible now. The investigation into Charlie's father, into my father, into lots of other families had begun. The Stone Cove Island I'd always known was truly gone forever.

I have to leave, I thought, staring at my house as we approached. *I can't stay here anymore.*

"I don't want to go in," I said when we got to the porch. I didn't know why. I sat down on the steps.

"Why don't I make us some tea?" Charlie asked.

He was too good to be true, really. But not really, I thought, because come January he'd be gone. What had happened to me? We had done everything we'd set out to do. We'd found Bess. We'd cleared Mom. But we'd erased every image I had of home. We'd stained every memory. Instead of a weight being lifted, I felt the fog pressing down on me too. I wanted to preserve the illusion of Stone Cove Island I'd always had.

Charlie came out with the tea. "Hey," he said, waving a thick manila envelope in his other hand. "It was on the kitchen counter." I took the tea and shook my head at the envelope.

"You open it. Thanks." The warm mug felt wonderful in my hands.

"You sure?"

I nodded.

He turned it over twice, then tore at the flap. It only took a second for him to glance over the letter. Then he turned back to me with a strange grin.

"Eliza," he said. "UCLA. I guess you really did apply."

I had forgotten all about it.

"I really did," I said. I looked at him, not understanding. "Early admission, actually . . ."

"Well, that's good. Because it would have been pretty weird if you hadn't. You know, seeing as you got accepted."

I'm not sure what happened next, other than Charlie sweeping me into his arms. The details that have stuck with me are just snapshots, like my memories of Hurricane Victor. I saw the scalding tea splash onto the front steps, the swirl of the beadboard ceiling above my head as Charlie swung me around the porch. I heard my own laughter and gasps of disbelief. But the image that really lingers was one I know existed solely in my mind. As I buried myself in Charlie's embrace, I saw the vivid flash of an anchor. Only this time, it wasn't a symbol, a threat, something to be hidden. It was attached to a boat, where it belonged. And it was finally being reeled in from the ocean floor.

ACKNOWLEDGMENTS:

Thank you to Dan Ehrenhaft, who is more creative kindred spirit than editor; to my always wise agent, Sarah Burnes; to go-to-girl Meredith Barnes and everyone at Soho Press.

Thank you to my friends who are such smart, tireless readers: Christie Colliopoulos, Laurie Shearing and especially Helen Thorpe, who held my hand all the way through my first novel. Thanks to KidLit 2. I can always count on you for inspiration and a good time.

Especially thank you to my husband, Adam, for your endless patience and excellent ideas.